Copyright © 2018 Samuel Jackson
All rights reserved
First Edition

PAGE PUBLISHING, INC.
New York, NY

First originally published by Page Publishing, Inc. 2018

ISBN 978-1-68409-450-9 (Paperback)
ISBN 978-1-68409-451-6 (Digital)

Printed in the United States of America

God's Love Speaks

SAMUEL JACKSON

Preface

The Meaning of The Cover Photo

We did not have our beginning, in the womb of our mother. We all had our original beginning, in the womb, of God's loving heart.

God who is love, created us, in His own image, after His own likeness, by and for himself. Love created us, by and for himself, to be love, even as God is.

Before the world, before our earthly parents, before all things born, God knew us, and called us, by our name,

God is calling us, back to the womb, of his loving heart, where we all first began. Let us fully fill our heart, with God who is love as we love God, even as God loves us. Let us be, heart to heart, with God. As God fills our heart, as we fill His heart.

Dedication

First and foremost, above and before all, I dedicate all, to the Lord my God. In whom, I live, move and breathe and have my very being.

Next, I dedicate this book and all I am, to my blessed, sweet, loving, angelic mother Larraine, better known as "Cookie". My inspiration who taught me to persist and persevere, through an attitude of gratitude. To endure and overcome every negative with a positive. I love you, Mom.

Next, I dedicate this book, and all I am, to my warrior father Samuel, who endured and overcame an abusive gambling, womanizing, alcoholic father growing up, who taught me courage, endurance, strength and perseverance. Who fought chest cancer and won. Who fought kidney cancer and won. Who fought bladder cancer and won. Who fought diabetes and high blood pressure and won. Who fought a major stroke and won. Who fought his final fight with liver cancer, and lost with grace and without complaint. Who left us Friday morning at 8:15 on July 17th 2015. We love and miss you Dad. Farewell my father and friend.

Next, I dedicate this book to my sister Debbie, a stage four breast cancer survivor. Love you, Sis.

Next, I dedicate this book, my heart, soul and life, to my faithful loving wife, Karen, who has always been my solid rock and sure foundation. Who settled me down and gave me deep roots, for once in my life. Who has always encouraged me and believed in me. Who never once gave up on me. Who has always stood behind me and beside me. My other self, my better self. Love you, Babe.

Next, I dedicate this book, my heart, soul and life, to my three sons: Cortney, David and Joshua. Dad loves you.

Next, I dedicate this book, my heart, soul and life equally to my two daughters: Danielle who has MS and Brittany. Dad loves you.

Next, I dedicate this book, my heart, soul and life, to my six grandsons: Hayden, Jacob, Bernan IV, Conner and my mixed grandson Malachi and to my grandson Carter Hayes. Papa loves you.

Next, I dedicate this book, my heart, soul and life, to my six granddaughters: Annabelle, Sophia, Lyla, Madison and Avery who was born over two months premature, and to my granddaughter Devyla Gould born 10 weeks early. Papa love you.

Next, I dedicate this book to my sons-in-law: Bernan III who gave me two granddaughters and two grandsons. To Jimmy who gave me one granddaughter and one grandson. To Todd who has given me one grandson.

Next I dedicate this book equally to my daughters-in-law: Stacy who gave me one granddaughter and one grandson, to Labrittany who gave me my mixed grandson Malachi. To Gabrielle who gave me two granddaughters.

I dedicate this book, and my deepest and sincerest heartfelt appreciation, thanks and gratitude to Casey Runyan, my publication Coordinator at Page Publishing Inc., in New York. Casey has gone way out of her way, far and above her call of duty to make this book the very best it can possibly be. Awesome and excellent job, Casey. You rock, girl. Together our names and work will travel the world, touching and transforming lives for generations to come. Sharing and spreading love, hope, peace, joy, wisdom and truth.

Finally, I dedicate this book, my heart, soul and life to all the readers of my book, "God's Love Speaks". My hope and prayer is that we become the very best of closest friends. That I may be your friend in the world and your brother in the Lord. Call, write to me, visit me anytime. Let's share our hearts, souls and lives together.

It is said and proven, one person can make a difference. One person can change the world. That one person begins with you. Together united as one, as that one, let's make a difference. Let's change the world. This book dedicated to the difference-makers and the world-changers.

Dedicated to all those who talk up, share and help promote by word of mouth, "God's Love Speaks". Together united by love, let's cause God's Love Speaks to take the world by storm, together let's plant love's seed, nurture it, help it produce a mighty harvest of love. Love is God's seed, for God is love.

I dedicate this book to love.

Dedicated to promoting the $35,000 a month need of the loving church I am an active participating member of "Beechwood Christian Church" on 12950 Easton ST NE, Alliance, Ohio 44601, at church phone number 330- 821-7602. 10% of all worldwide sales of "God's Love Speaks" and 100% of my next book "God's Love Speaks" goes to "Beechwood Christian Church" towards spreading the gospel of Jesus Christ worldwide, and reaching and saving of lost souls for Christ worldwide. Help us spread the gospel and to save lost souls, by promoting this book, with everyone you meet, know and love, by word of mouth and ask everyone to do the same.

Dedicated to the Senior Pastor of "Beechwood Christian Church," my loving brother in the Lord and best friend in the world "Mark Black".

Dedicated to all of the extremely friendly and loving congregation members at "Beechwood Christian Church" Who's hearts over abundantly, overflow with love for God, and the love of God for their fellow mankind. A loving family of God, who welcomes, accepts, and love everyone just as they are and not as they ought to be. Members overflowing with patience, kindness, mercy, forgiveness, generosity, and understanding. Loving souls I am proud and honored, to call my fellow brothers and sisters, in the family of God,

Dedicated to those seeking a church home.

Dedicated to encouraging fellow believers in our Lord Jesus Christ, to come and fellowship with us at "Beechwood Christian Church," anytime you are in our area. We would be proud and honored, to meet you and to personally get to know and love you. We invite you to journey with us, side by side, hand in hand, and heart to heart, on our way to God's promised glory land, before the throne and face of God our Heavenly Father. As he calls us all, to come back home to him, at the end of life's journey. Where the tree of life does blossom, the river of life does flow, the angels sing and the saints do praise him, who is faithful and true. Where perfect love abounds, and perfect peace and joy are found. Come walk with us as we walk with the Lord. We will see you soon and often, if it be the Father's perfect will and good pleasure. God and we ourselves are here for you always. Pray for us always, as we always pray for you and yours, to be safe and sound.

Introduction

In 1 John 4:8, it is written, God is love.

In Genesis 1:26-27, it is written, God (He who is love), created both male and female in His image, after His likeness.

Mankind was created by love, to be loved, to love God, to love others, to be loved by God, and by others.

God's Love Speaks is a collection of heavenly inspired poems, written by Devine Design. Messages from God's loving heart, through the author's loving heart, to your loving heart.

Outward expressions of God's inward love for Heaven and earth, and the fullness thereof.

Even as we love God, because God first loved us. Even so, others will love us, because we first love them.

Jesus said, "A new commandment I give you, that you love one another, the same as I love you."

As a living soul, we are the earthly loving home, of Heaven's Living Love. Where Heaven's Living Love, fully lives in us, fully reigns supreme over us and continuously and unconditionally flows forth through us, unto one another.

Hate, the absence of love, only triumphs, when loving souls do nothing and speak not. Thus comes "God's Love Speaks", speaking love loud and clear. Let "God's Love" speak to you, through you, unto others. Share and spread heaven's love.

When these poems speak to you, use them to lovingly speak to others.

Before we can reap a harvest of love, we must first sow the seeds of love into the fertile soil of the heart, soul, mind and life of others.

Everyone desires, needs and wants to be loved. Always be love and everyone will always desire, need, want and love you. Love everyone, family, friend and foe, equally. As no respector of persons, like God.

"These inspired poems, will enlighten your mind to put on the mind of Christ, will touch your heart with the loving heart of God, will stir your soul to have God's Love fill your soul, and could change your life to be conformed to the image and likeness of God's Dear Son."

We are all in continuous search for absolute, pure, perfect, unchanging, unconditional love. An eternal foundation upon which to base and build our daily lives. Only God, who crested us, in His image, and after his likeliness (Gen 1:26-27), is such love (1 John 4:8). God who is such love, seeks to over abundantly fill us with Himself, to past overflowing. Until only He who is such love, remains in us, and reigns over us, flows forth through us, unto all those around us. Let us, as children born of God who is Love, be Love even as God is love. That may be all that God created and intended us to be. Children born of Love to be Love, born to love God and others, born to be loved by God and others. Even as we love God because God first loved us, even so, let others love us, because we first love them. Before we can reap an abundant harvest of love, we must first abundantly sow the seeds of love. As we do sow, so do we also reap. Receive, Be, Share, God's love.

POEMS ABOUT LOVE

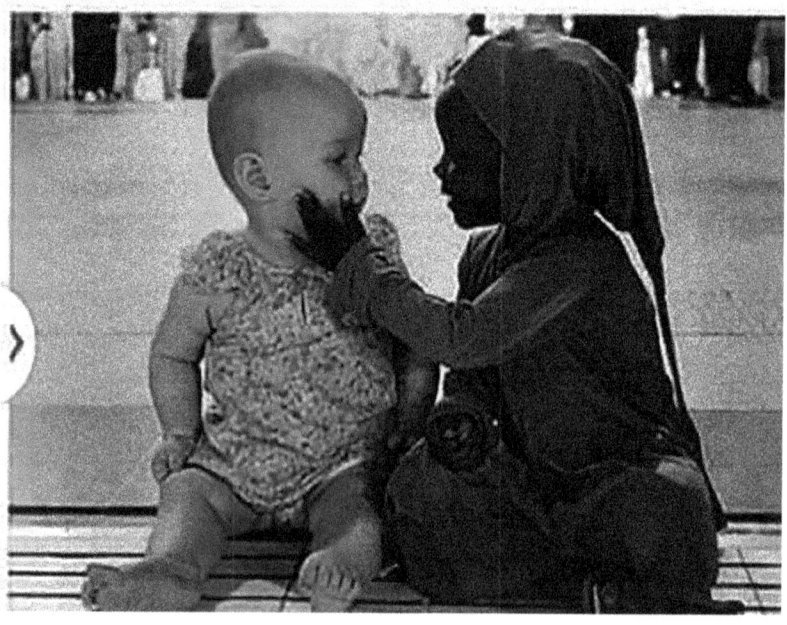

"All Lives Matter"

God made You, God made Me,
Not our Color, Does God see;

Search deep Inside, Look Deep Within,
To find The Image, made like Him;

Some are Black, Some are White,
But ALL are Precious, in God's sight;

Small minded ones, they cannot see,
God's Perfect Love, that sets Us Free;

They ONLY see, the Color of skin,
But fail to see, The Soul Within;

Who are we, to judge another,
Can any soul, choose their color;

By color of skin, let us Not judge,
Instead sow seeds, of Peace and Love;

Let peace abound, between Us ALL,
As we answer to, Love's Highest Call;

We Must learn, to get along,
To keep us safe, to make us strong;

As equal members, of the human race,
Let's make OUR world, a Better Place;

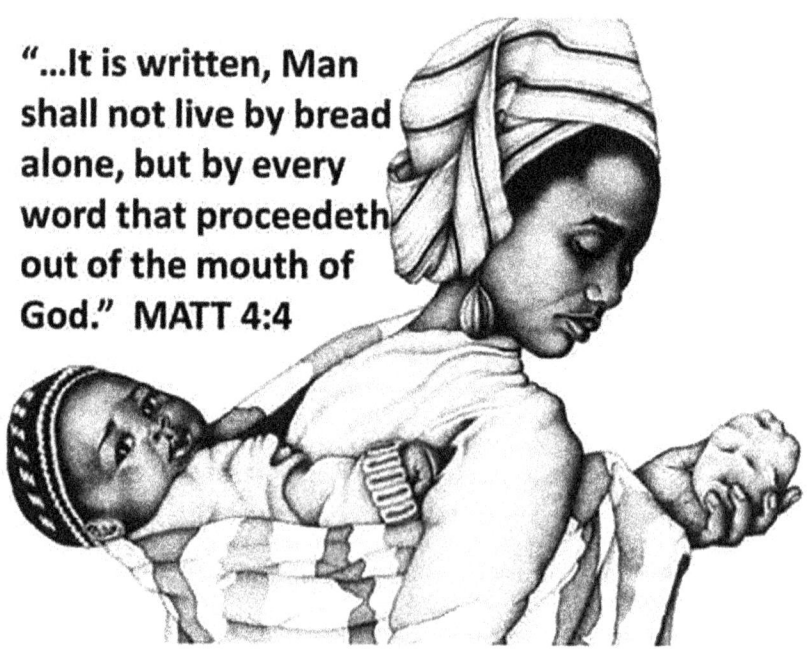

"...It is written, Man shall not live by bread alone, but by every word that proceedeth out of the mouth of God." MATT 4:4

"Eternal Pie"

I'd start out with a special bowl,
That none can buy or sell;

The bowl is every living soul,
Where God Almighty Dwells:

I'd pour in abundant joy,
Then add, God's perfect Love:

Add the Peace, that will not cease,
From the Heart of God Above;

I'd add in some delicious fruits,
The Fruits of God's Dear Spirit;

Then I'd add God's Holy Word,
Then pray that all would hear it;

I'd add lots of quiet time,
So we may stop to pray;

Add in God's forgiveness,
For the sins we do each day:

I'd add Heavenly revelations,
To make God's dreams come true;

To be conformed to God's Dear Son,
God's destiny for me and you;

I'd blend it together with God's grace,
Then name it, Eternal Pie;

I'd serve it to the human race,
And feed the world and I;

* Jesus said <u>IF</u> you love me (The word who is God and Christ the Son of God) Feed my lambs (The Babes in Christ The Word) Who desires the Sincere milk of the word, Feed my Sheep (The mature in Christ the word), with the meat of the word. *

L is patient
is kind
does not envy
does not boast
is not proud
is not rude
O is not self-seeking
is not easily angered
V keeps no record of wrongs
does not delight in evil
rejoices with the truth
always protects
E always trusts
always hopes
always perseveres
never fails

1 Corinthian

"Love, God's Free Gift"

Love is what we make of it,
We must first give of ourselves;

It matters not, if we are poor,
For love is the Wealth of wealth;

Love comes not from money,
Love comes from God above;

Love is God's free gift to us,
So let us freely love;

Worry not that you'll have no love,
Because you give it all away;

For the Love you'll reap tomorrow,
Is the Love you sow today:

LOVE

That one word sums up all Jesus said for us to do. If you'll build your life on it, even the most violent storms of this world will be unable to shake you. It will make you solid in every area of your life.

"Love, An Eternal Symphony"

Love is not an ownership,
Bought buy a band of gold;

Love, an eternal friendship,
Life's treasure to behold;

Love knows no age nor bounds,
Love is forever young and free;

Love is full of joyous sounds,
God's Eternal Symphony;

With God as the Conductor,
Who directs with hands of Love;

Who keeps us all in harmony,
As He listens from above;

"Love One Another"

Love seeks not to serve itself,
Love strives to serve another;

We must learn, to love ourselves,
Before we can love, each other;

"Love was not meant, for us to keep',
"Nor placed in our heart, to stay";

"It's said, Love isn't really Love",
"Until we give our love away";

Worry not that you'll have no love,
As you give your love away;

For the love you'll reap tomorrow,
Is the Love you sow Today;

"The Golden Rule"

* As we sow unto others, even so we reap unto ourselves. Some 10, some 20, some 100 fold. Therefore, sow peace, truth, and love, that you may reap the fullness of the fruits thereof, unto yourself. Love those who hates you. Bless those who curses you. Make peace with those who wars against you. Give to those who steals from you. We reap not as others sow unto us. But as we sow unto one another. *

"Love A Complete Commitment"

Love, a complete commitment,
Until death, do we part:

Not just married, by the courts,
But married, in our heart:

Love's a perfect unison,
Two hearts, are joined as one:

Love is complete forgiveness,
For any wrongs, we've done:

Love is not, mere sex in bed,
Nor is it, where love starts:

For lust, is merely, of the head,
While love, is of our hearts:

Date someone who wants to chase God with you.

"The Honesty Of Love"

Love is always honest,
Love is based on trust;

Love is for the Inward Soul,
And never outward lust;

Love is Never deceitful,
Love cannot live with lies;

For Love based on dishonesty,
Is a Love that quickly dies;

Love is unconditional,
Love Loves me just for me;

Love accepts us as we are,
Not as we ought to be;

"Unfaithfulness"

You cheated and lied,
You defiled our bed;

You failed to honor,
The vows you said;

To forsake all others,
To be Faithful and True;

To be open and honest,
In ALL that you do;

You violated my trust,
You broke my heart;

It's time I move on,
To make a new start;

My Love I forgive you,
For ALL you've done;

As I follow the footsteps,
Of God's Only Son;

"The Power of Love"

It's Love that can enslave us,
Or Love can set us free;

Love can lead us to our victory,
Or drive us to our knees;

To our knees so we may pray,
For a Loved one or a friend;

For God to help in times of need,
To save them in the end;

Love can be rewarding,
Love is not in vain;

As we recall with fondness,
The memories that remain;

"The Eternal Gates Of Glory"

The Eternal Gates Of Glory,
Are Now, Swung Open Wide;

We Enter Our Father's Presence,
As His Spotless Bride;

The Saints. Are All Rejoicing,
The Angels Sing Their Song:

Before The Lord, Upon His Throne,
To Him, Do We Belong;

The Tree Of Life, Does Blossom,
The Fountain Of Youth, Does Flow;

The Light Of God Is Shinning,
His Peace, Does Flood Our Soul;

Our Joy, Is Over Abundant,
We Answer To, Truth's Call,

God's Love, Is Unconditional,
That Fills The Heart, Of All;

The End.

"Beyond The Veil"

Help Us Peer, Beyond The Veil,
Of The Man, Whom We Did See;

To Know And See, The Unknown God,
Who came To Set Us Free;

Help Us Receive, The Logos,
God's Pre Existing Son;

For It Is He, Whose Lord Of ALL,
With Him, May We Be One;

The End

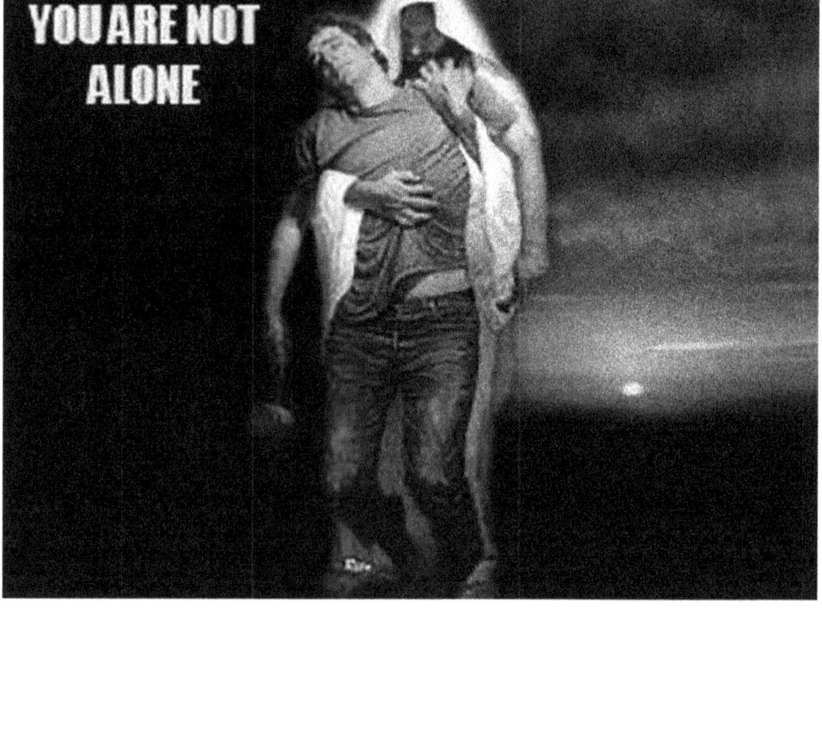
YOU ARE NOT
ALONE

"I'm Spiritually Lonely"

I Miss You Lord,
So Very Much;

These Trials Of Life,
Are Really Tough;

Be My Strength,
Make Me Strong;

I Cannot Do This,
On My Own;

I.m Spiritually Lonely,
Having No Equal;

To Help Me Fight,
Against ALL This Evil;

Send Me Just One,
Who Understands;

The Bigger Picture,
Of The Master's Plan;

Do Everything In Love

Sending Love your way
Today, Tomorrow
and Always.

"Love, The Crown of crowns"

Love seeks Not, to serve Itself,
But Always, to serve Another;

Without the seeking, of rewards,
A world of sin, Love covers;

Love makes us feel, Like Kings & Queens,
For Love is, the Crown of crowns;

Love elevates us, to Highest heights,
When we're feeling blue or down;

Love, leads us unto Victory,
Against our every foe;

As we love our enemies,
And All the ones we know;

HUMAN RELATIONSHIP POEMS

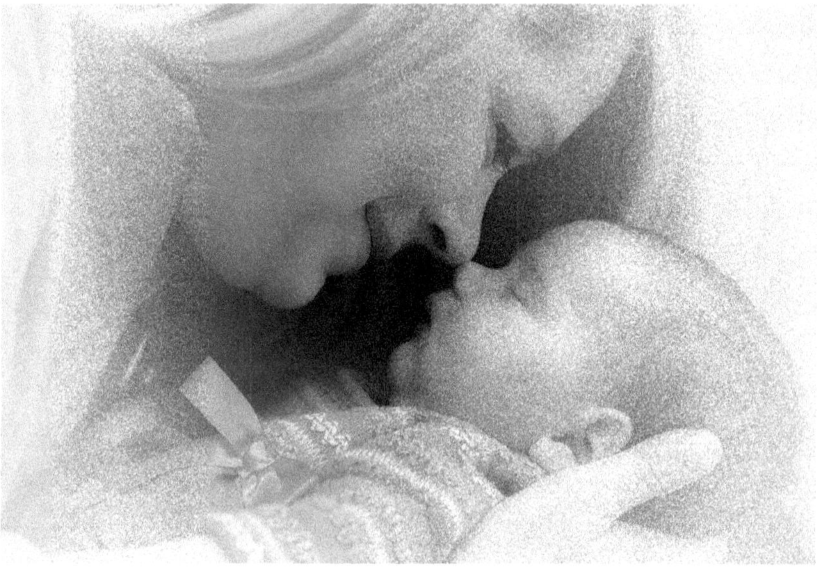

"God's Gifts To Me"

When they were born, as Brand New Babes,
A moment cherished, a treasure saved;

We see their first smile, hear their first cry,
We wipe their tear drops, from their eyes;

We watch them crawl, then walk, then run,
Lots of hours, filled with lots of fun;

The joy we hear, when first they speak,
We laugh, we play, we tickle their feet;

Soon, their childhood, comes then goes,
As they mature, we help them grow;

They will grow up, but they'll always be,
My precious Angels, God's Gifts to me;

Shower your children, with Daily love,
For they are Your gifts, from God Above;

* Train up a child, in peace, love, and Joy, and when they are old, when they mature, they will not depart, from peace, love, and joy. For peace, love and joy, are the ways they ought to go and grow *

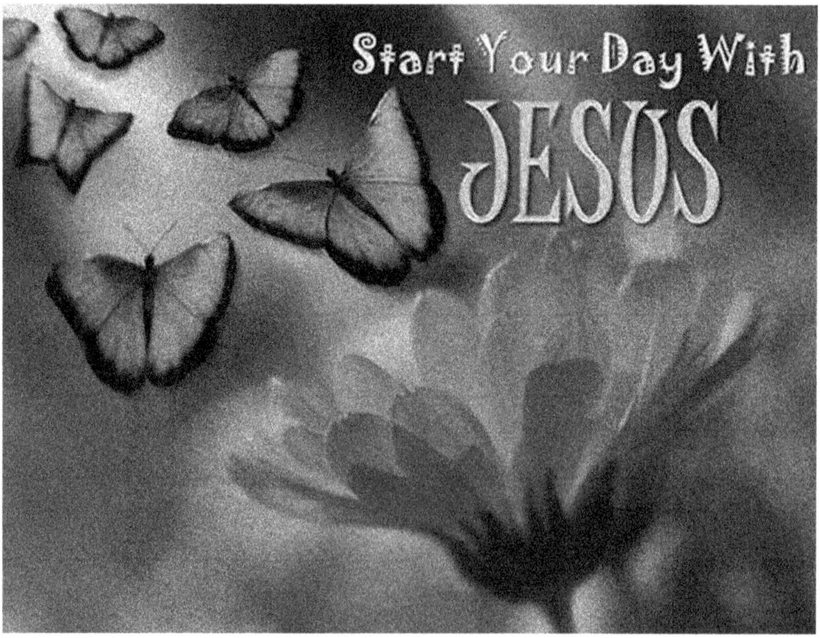
Start Your Day With
JESUS

"Sowing Seeds of Peace and Joy"

Our best, is never good enough,
As ALL, will come to know;

So many things, unsaid and done,
When it comes, our time to go;

If Only, I were young again,
Different seeds, I would sow;

I'd sow the seeds, of peace and joy,
Nurtured with Love, to help them grow;

We can't turn back, the hands of time,
It's said, What's done is done"

So learn to do, your best in life,
And do It, while you're young;

One thing, do I always pray for,
One thing, my forever goal;

The Lord of the harvest, will use me,
Te reap for Him, Lost souls;

---

* His perfect peace, the Prince of Peace, gives unto us that surpasses all understanding, all logic, rhyme, and reasoning. Blessed are the peacemakers, who brings forth the Prince of Peace, who gives others his perfect through his peace makers for they shall be called, the children of God. Full of the Son of God. *

~ PREPARE YOUR HEART ~
Look
Jesus is Coming
With the clouds
And every eye
Will see Him ...
Revelation 1:7

"On Earth As It Is In Heaven"

A world of souls, free of fear,
A world, at perfect peace;

As we sow, the seeds of Love,
God's Joy, that will Not cease;

Loving souls, who thinks of others,
Not merely, of themselves alone;

Giving souls, who fills another's needs,
Is the strength, that keeps us strong;

Helping souls, lands a helping hand,
A smile, and acts of kindness;

Let's make our world, a better place,
When we leave the world, behind us;

* As a person sows, so do they also reap. We reap not what others sow unto us, but what we sow in return unto others. Therefore sow love unto those who sows hate. They will reap the hate they sow unto themselves, you will reap love unto yourself. Sow peace in times of war. Sow truth in the presence of lies. Sow blessings, when others sow curses. Sow light, when others sow darkness. Sow joy when others sow sorrow. You reap what you sow, unto yourself. Seeds you sow, are the harvests you reap. *

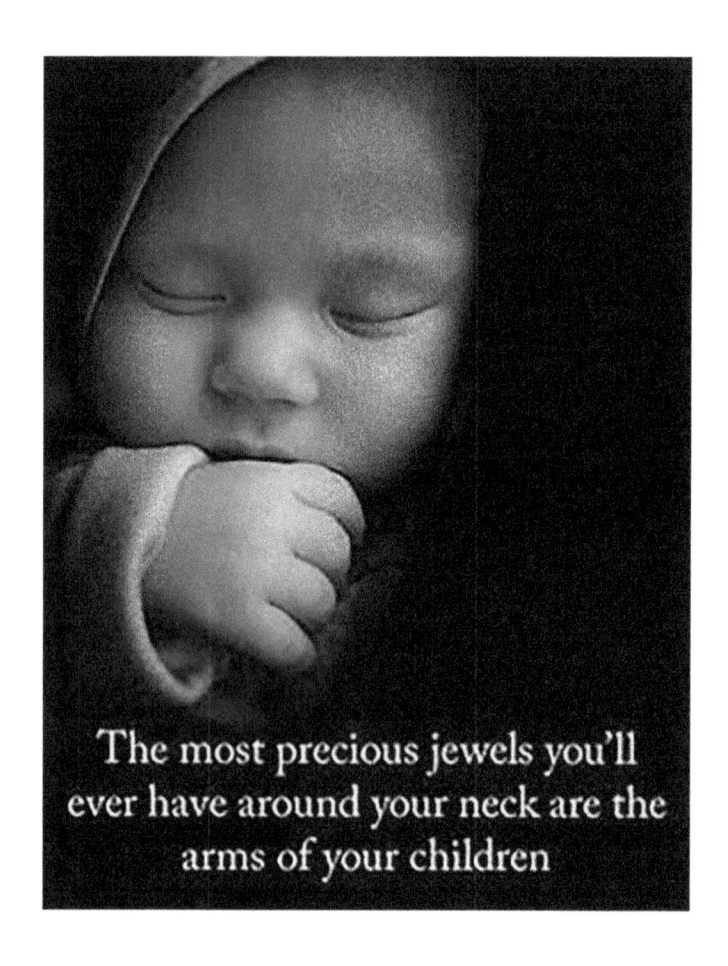

> The most precious jewels you'll ever have around your neck are the arms of your children

"Life's Treasure Chest"

When this life, is done and over,
I can say, I did my best;

As I recall, the precious jewels,
From Life's treasure chest;

The Jewels, of love and laughter,
Shared, with family and friends;

Treasures, in the life hereafter,
When I reach, my journey's end;

Be sure to say, I Love You,
Do the acts. of kindness;

Leave the world, a better place,
As we leave the world, behind us;

POEMS ABOUT GOD

You have MY SPIRIT

The Token of MY Love

"Come Holy Spirit"

Come Holy Spirit, fill this place,
Fill us Fully, With God's Grace;

Shine God's Glory, upon our face,
Give us strength, to run our race;

When Jesus comes, and passes by,
Let us walk, close by His side;

Hand in hand, and heart to heart,
From God's Truth, we don't depart;

We cannot make it, without Christ,
For He alone, is our Breath of Life;

Give us Your power, to overcome,
Help us defeat, the wicked one;

---

* The wicked, whom God is angry with everyday (Psalm 7:11). Whom God turns into hell, into the absence of the eternal presence of the eternal God (Psalm 9:17). Are they who has not God (the word John 1:1 Christ the second person in heaven (John 5:7 KJV). In <u>ALL</u> of their thoughts (Psalm 10:4) Those who has not put on the mind of Christ (Phil 2:5). Those who have not brought all of their thoughts into captivity (Held Prisoner) unto the obedience of Christ (of the word who is God)* of the inward spirit man from above (Col 1:27)

Fire of God, burn within me!

"Set Our Soul On Fire"

Look down, O Lord, lift us up,
Out of the muck and mire;

Shower us, with The Holy Spirit,
And set our soul, on fire;

Help us, turn the world, upside down,
Which would make it, right side up;

Your Will be done, the lost be won,
Lord, let this be our cup;

"Once lost, but now we're found",
"Once blind, but now we see";

Sin nor death, can hold us down,
For we have been, set free:

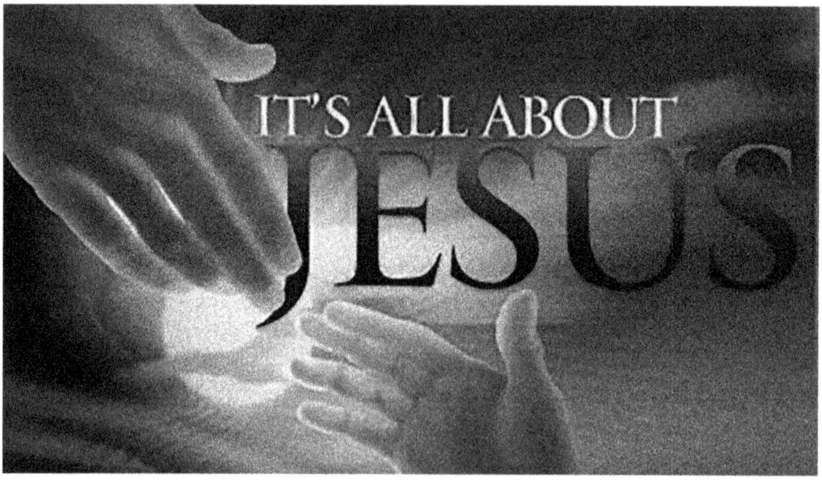
IT'S ALL ABOUT
JESUS

"Our Blessed Savior"

Christ descended, from God above,
To share with us, our Father's Love;

Born in a manger, as but a babe,
Our Savior born, on Christmas day;.

Wise men led, by His bright star,
Came to worship, how great Thou are;

Christ in the likeness, of mortal men,
Came to break, our chains of sin;

Christ Lived, then died, our sins to pay,
But then the stone, was rolled away;

Then Christ Arose, for All to see,
For hell and death, could Not hold He;

Christ Ascended, to God's Right Hand,
Upon His Throne, where He began;

Christ, our Resurrection, and our Life,
Our bridegroom, Who loves His Wife;

Christ is returning, soon someday,
To come and take, His Bride away;

The Marriage supper, of The Lamb,
At the table's head, The Great I Am;

From All our sins, we do refrain,
Into Christ's image, we are changed;

In God's Kingdom, we eternal dwell,
Christ has saved, our soul from hell;

To Heaven above, we ever remain,
We sing with angels, In Jesus name;

The angels sing, the saints rejoice,
Our Father Speaks, His pure sweet Voice;

O Lion of Judah, we hear You roar,
From sea to sea, from shore to shore;

We will walk, God's Street of gold,
With All God's saints, from days of old;

With Pearly Gate, swung open wide,
Our Father calls, to come inside;

Here's the beauty, of our Father's plan,
Our mansion awaits us, in glory land;

God's eternal Presence, our destiny,
As He awaits, for you and me;

The Lord of lords, the King of kings,
Our Breath of Life, our Everything;

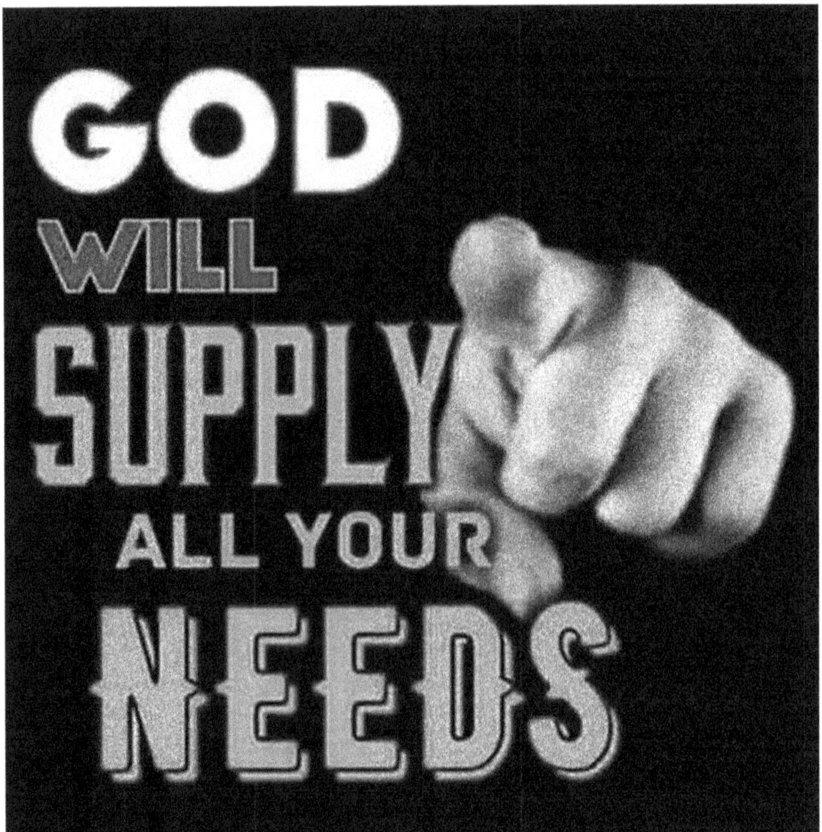
GOD
WILL
SUPPLY
ALL YOUR
NEEDS

"God Is Our Provider"

When we're without, our God provides,
ALL the things we need;

For God is Ever, by our side,
We are His child, His seed;

God's our Shelter, when we have no home,
Under His Wings, we safely dwell;

God's our Companion, when alone,
In the depths of deepest hell;

When we're naked, our Lord clothes us,
He heals us, when we're ill;

It's God Who fills, the void within,
Which Only God can Fill;.

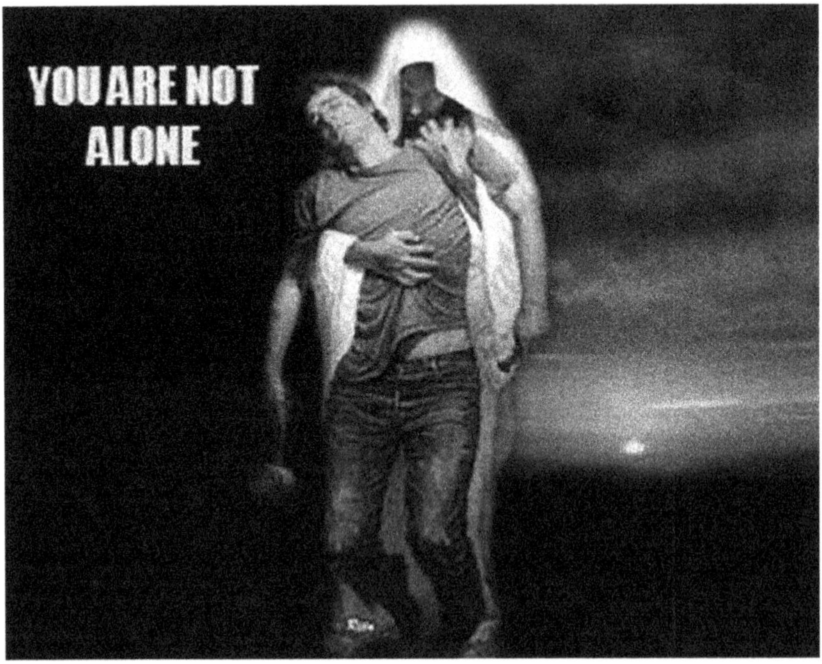
YOU ARE NOT
ALONE

"God Is Forever Near"

Have faith and courage, to face each day,
For this is the day, our Lord has made;

Believe in God, Believe in Yourself,
Place Not your faith, upon a shelf;

for faith without works, is dead,
You Must work your faith, to succeed;

Heed Not the doubts, or fears in your head,
But with ALL your heart, believe;

You are Never, alone my child,
ALL will work out right;

If You'll Always walk by faith.
And Never walk by sight;

God dwells within His Kingdom,
His Kingdom dwells in us:

God is In Us, where we are,
In Him, we place us our;

* (Luke 17:21) The kingdom of God (of the word John 1:1, the light of life in us John 1:1, 4, 9, of Christ in us Gal 4:19, Col 1:27, 29, Eph 3:14-17, Of he who is the light of life John 8:12), is not here or there, (Is not somewhere outside ourselves), but is within us *

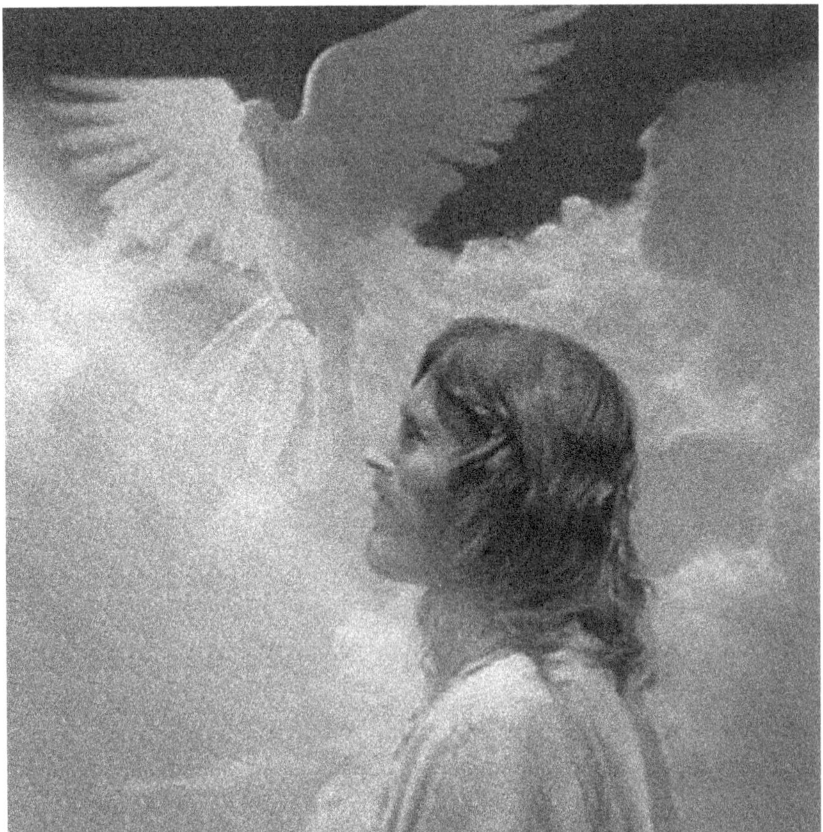

"Our Maker In Disguise"

You are a God sent blessing,
Our Maker In Disguise;

We're proud, we are the ones, You chose,
For us, You chose to die;

Lord we need You, and we want You,
This is plain to see;

You're Everything, we've dreamed of,
The Truth, Who sets us Free;

Lord we love You, with ALL our heart,
With ALL our soul and mind;

We pray O Lord, You Never part,
You are the Peace we find;

You are our Lord, our Savior,
You are our God, our King;

With You may we find favor,
For You are our Everything;

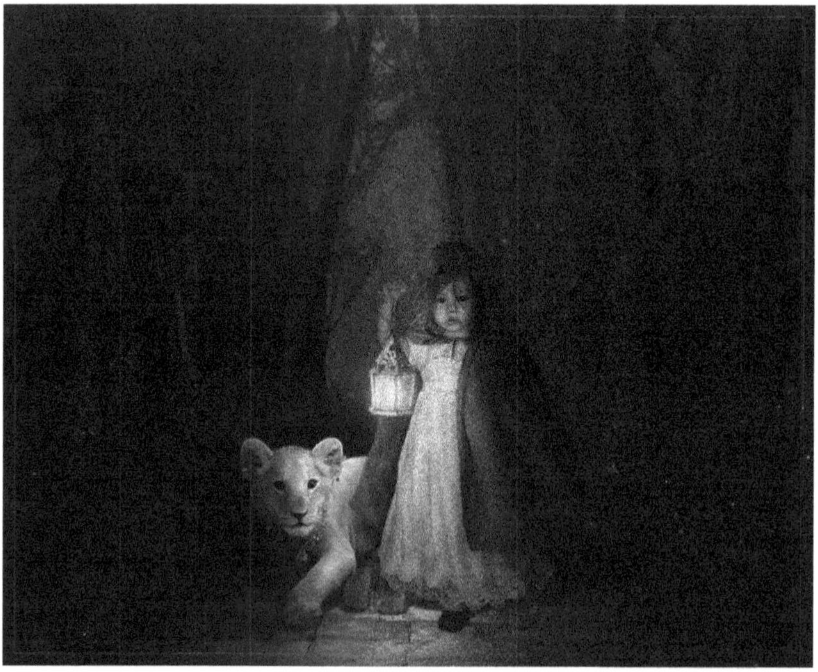

"Christ Is Our Guiding Light"

God's our Warmth, when we are cold,
He's our Protection, from all things;

He'll be our Strength, when we are old,
He's the Song of Joy we sing;

In God, we have a Perfect Peace,
Throughout, the day and night;

In God our lives, are so complete,
Christ is our Guiding Light;

So why fear, what men can do,
Or even what men may say;

We follow Christ, Whose love is True,
The Truth, The Life, The Way;

* Christ, the word who is God and the only begotten Son of God, the second person who bears record in heaven (John 1:1, John 5:7 KJV), is the light of life (John 8:12), who is in every living soul who enters the world (John 1:1, 4, 9). The same Christ the word, who is in us (Gal 4:19, Col 1:27, 29, Eph 3:14-17). For the word, God's Son who created heaven and earth (psalm 33:6, Heb 1:2, 3), the world and all things (John 1:1-3) By and for himself (Col 1:15-17), is the breath of life (Acts 17:24, 25, 28), God breathes into our nostrils, to cause us to become, be and remain a living soul (Gen 2:7), *

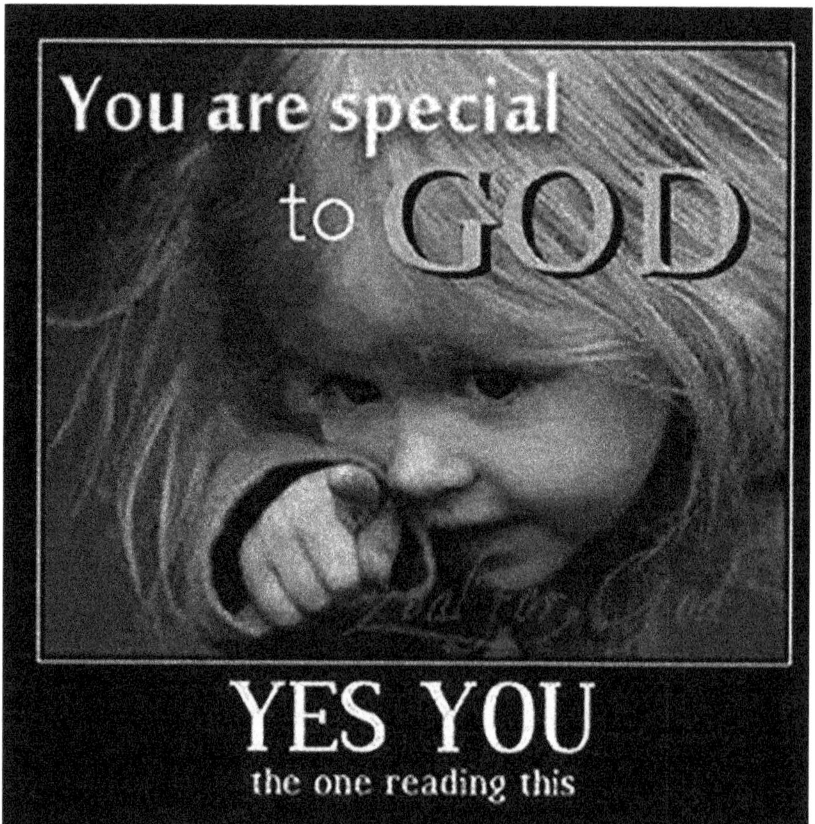
You are special
to GOD
YES YOU
the one reading this

"Our Father Speaks"

Our Father Speaks, His Eternal Voice,
Upon the sound, our soul rejoice;

Let us Remember, Let us recall,
Our Father's Voice, Created All;

God Speaks His Voice, we have our Breath,
Without God's Voice, there's only death;

Through God's Voice, we do exist,
Our Father's Voice, we don't resist;

We hide His Voice, within our heart,
From His Voice, we won't depart;

His Voice calls out, come follow Me,
I am The Truth, Who sets you free;

Our chains of sin, have now been broken,
Through The Son, God's Word Spoken;

* God the Father said, spoke forth his word, his voice Christ the only begotten Son, and the heavens and earth, were created (Gen 1:1, Psalm 33:6, John 1:1-3, 10, 11). The same voice Adam heard walking in the garden, but hid himself form (Gen 3:8, 10), The same voice who created the world, who is our breath of life (Acts 17:24, 25, 28), whom we hear walking in the garden of our soul (John 1:1, 4, 9), we hide ourselves in. *

The Lord
will fight for you,
you need only to
be still

Exodus 14:14

"God Is Our Avenger"

(This Poem I wrote because of the 9/11 terrorist attacks)

Others may take, our life from us,
But this, they cannot steal'

Our faith in God, in Whom we trust,
His Perfect Peace, we feel;

Our God is Our Avenger,
He, defeats our foes;

In times of present danger,
God is the strength we know;

God gathers us All together,
For us to stand as one;

God will forget us never,
Through Christ, His Only Son;

It's no longer, we who lives,
But Christ, Who lives Within;

Christ our Way, Whom God gives,
Who breaks our chains of sin;

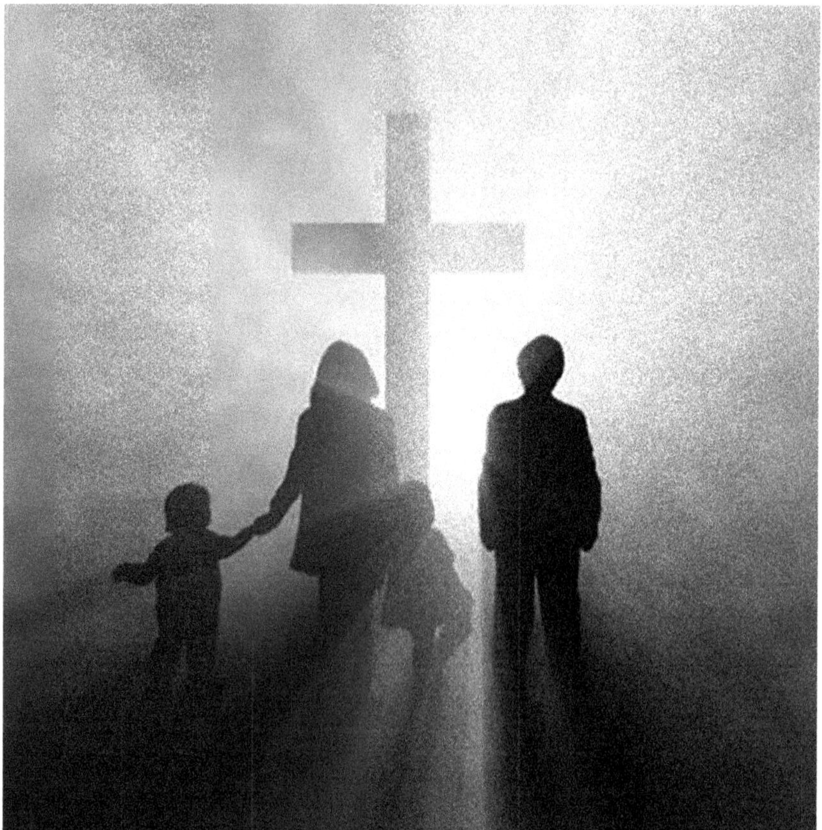

"Lead Thou Us On"

Now we search, Within Ourselves,
For God's eternal peace;

There we find eternal wealth,
And joy that will not cease;

God comforts us, when we're weary,
When we feel we can't go on;

We hear His Voice speak clearly,
God's strength will keep us strong;

God will lead us on to victory,
God will fight our foes:

As God has done through history,
For ALL who loves Him so;

Greater is Christ Within us,
Then All who are in the world;

In God Alone we place our trust,
By Whom the worlds unfurled;

(The reason for the choice of picture the Author chose for this poem, is in hopes, that we are all led to the cross, which is the power of our salvation, as we daily pick up our cross, mortifying the lusts and deeds of our flesh, in order to follow our Lord in the Spirit, as we are led by the Spirit (Romans 8; 14), as ones born of the Spirit (John 3; 5- 7), and not by the flesh (Romans 8;1, Ephesians 4; 22 - 24, Gal. 5; 16) !

Riches and Honor are with ME; Enduring Wealth and Righteousness.

Proverbs 8:18

"Our God Never Fails"

Why should we worry, doubt, or fret,
For our troubles Cannot last;

Our God has NEVER failed us yet,
God's Love for us Stands Fast;

When our body, is dead and gone,
And they lay us in the grave;

Our Inner Man will live on,
For we know God's Word saves;

Through God's Word, God's Only Son,
Who warns us to repent;

Through God's Word, we Know we've Won,
For our Savior, Has been sent;

* The word is the second person who bears record in heaven with God the father and the holy spirit, the son of God (1 John 5:7), who was with God in the beginning as god (John 1:1), who is eternal (1 Peter 1:23), Who cannot die or pass away (Matt 24:35). Who cannot return unto the Father void (Isa 55:11). Who created the world and all things (John 1:3), who was in the world (John 1:10, 11), Whom we bear record of (1 John 1:1, 2), Who is the Lord of all (Acts 10:36, 37), And the Lord of lords (Rev 19:13, 16), Who is our breath of life (Acts 17:24, 25, 28), Whom God Breathes into our nostrils (Gen 2:7), Whom God sends to heal and deliver us (Psalm 107:19-20), Who is able to save our soul (James 1:21). The Christ in us (Gal 4:19, Col 1:27, 29, Eph 3:14-17).

And the Word
was made flesh,
and dwelt
among us,
and we
beheld
His glory...
John 1:14

"God's Word"

God's Word our King,
Sits on our throne;

God's Word our Way,
Who leads us home;

God's Word our Truth,
Who sets us Free:

God's Word our Light,
By Whom we See;

God's Word our Healer,
Who makes us whole;

God's Word our Savior,
Who saves our soul;

God's Word our Water,
Who quenches our Thirst;

God's Word our Treasure,
Whom we seek First;

God's Word our Provider,
Who provides our needs;

God's Word is God's Son,
The Father's Good Seed;

God's Word our Protector,

Who conquers our foes;

God's Word our Companion,
Wherever we go;

God's Word our Creator,
Who created us All;

God's Word is our Rock,
We Cannot fall;

God's Word our Bread,
Who feeds us each day;

God's Word our Shepherd,
Who shows us The Way;

God's Word is God's Love,
Whom we freely give;

God's Word gives us Faith,
By Whom we live;

God's Word our Strength,
When we are weak;

God's Word is our God,
Whom we daily seek;

God's Word our Breath,
Who gives us Life;

God's Word our Hero,
Each day and night;

POEMS ABOUT OUR RELATIONSHIP WITH GOD

THE FAVOR OF GOD IS AT YOUR DOOR!

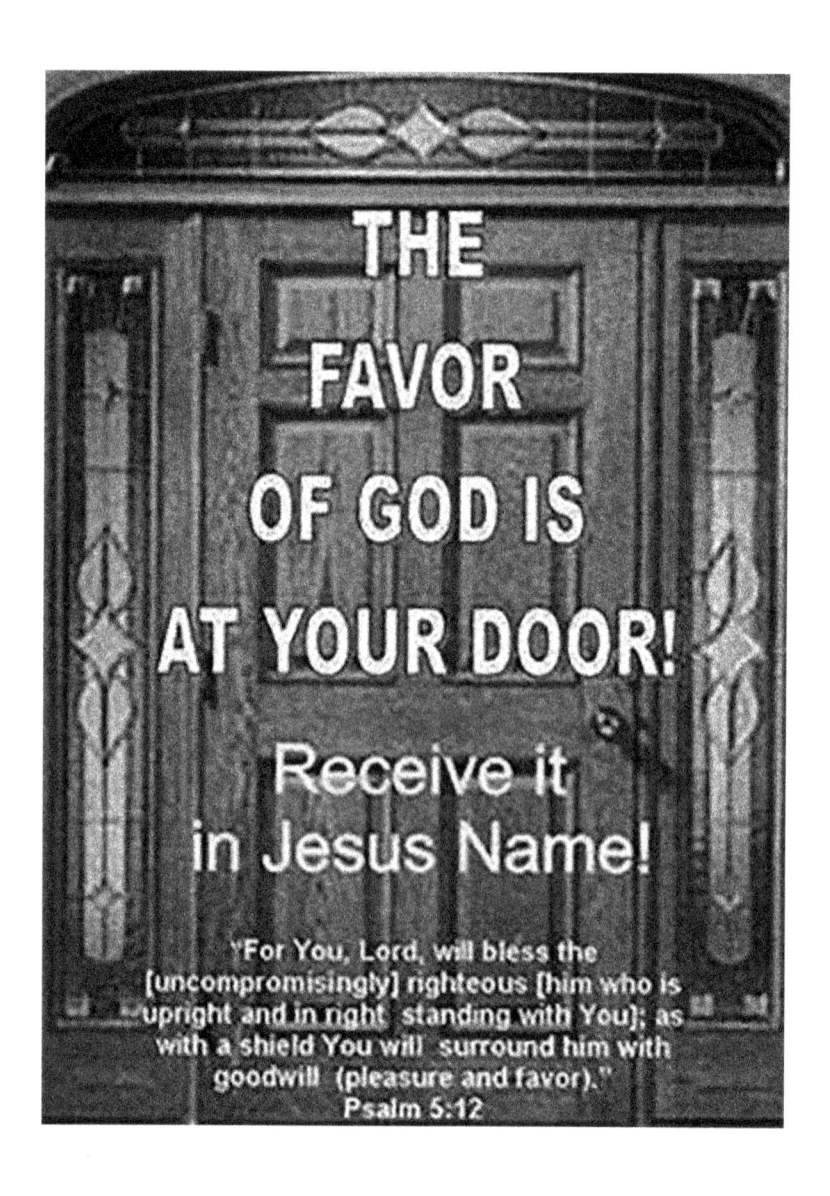

Receive it in Jesus Name!

"For You, Lord, will bless the [uncompromisingly] righteous [him who is upright and in right standing with You]; as with a shield You will surround him with goodwill (pleasure and favor)."
Psalm 5:12

"The Lord Is Knocking"

Christ knocked, upon my heart's door,
And I joyfully welcomed Him in;

He said to me, go and sin nor more,
For I broke your chains of sin;

I came, I lived, then died for you,
Then I raised up from the grave;

So you may be born a new,
For I am He Who saves;

I am The Way, The Truth, and Life,
The Light by which you see;

I am the end of All your strife,
The Truth Who sets you Free;

* (John 17:17) Sanctify them through God's truth (Christ John 14:6, The word of God who is God and the only Son of God), Your word O God, is truth. You shall know (fully comprehend and understand) The truth Christ the word who is the son of God, and the truth (God's son the word), will set you free indeed –for they whom the son (The word, the truth) sets free, is free indeed *

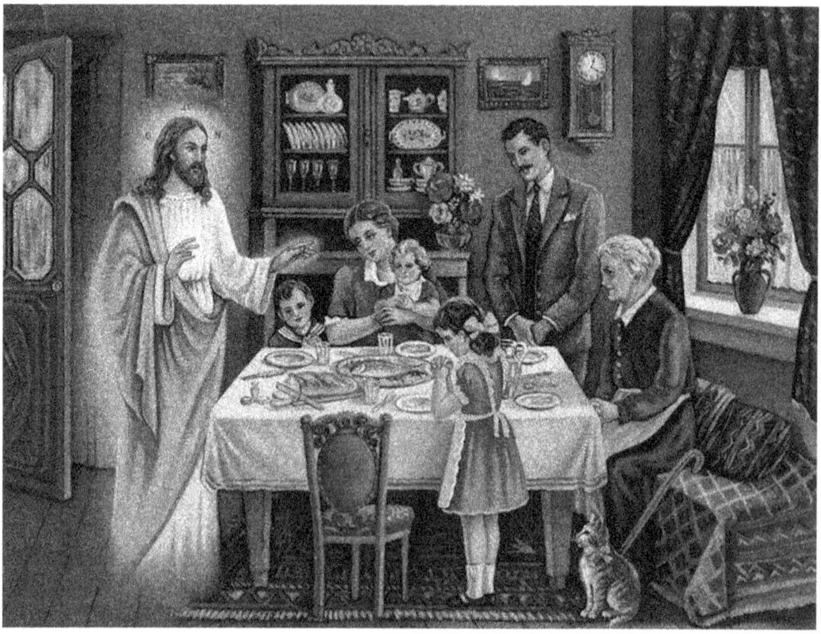

"At Home With God"

Teach me Lord, that we're Not Alone,
Within our heart, You made Your Home;

Teach us O Word, Who gives us Faith,
To seek You in our Secret Place;

Deep in the secrecy of our heart,
There we know, our Faith Must start;

Teach us O Lord, to be Not Deceived,
Not to seek signs, but to only believe;

To believe in You, More than ourselves,
To seek God's face, Before God's wealth;

Fill our heart, make us pure,
Give us strength and courage, to endure;

Make our Heart pure, through God's Grace,
So we may behold, God's Loving Face;

---

* Blessed are the pure in heart, those whose heart, (thoughts, desires, intents), are full to overflowing with the abundance of every pure word of God, we hide in our heart (Psalm 119:11), for they shall see (fully know and understand) God (he who is the word our creator John 1:1-3) we know him, when he fills our heart with himself

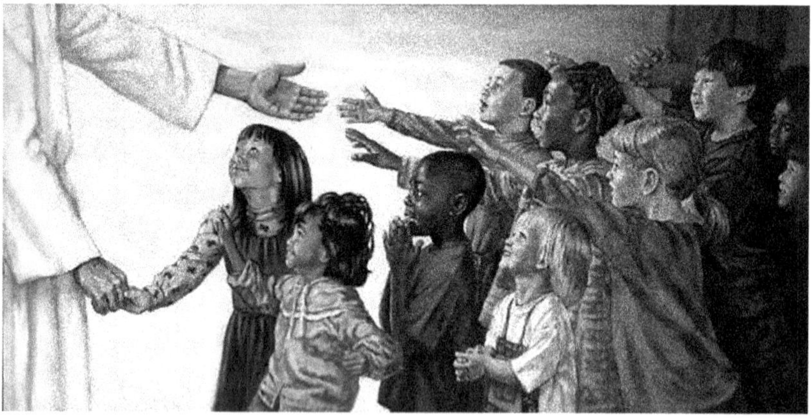

"The Master And I"

Hand in hand, The Master and I,
Return to The Father of Lights;

There shall we forever dwell,
No more to say Goodnight;

Heart to heart, and side by side,
We dwell forever, united as one;

As God reveals, to my wondering eyes,
All the miracles, Gad has done;

Let my enemies come against me,
For I will Never fear;

When they take this mortal life,
Then I will leave them here;

God's Kingdom isn't here nor there,
God's Kingdom is Within;

So why fear I, what the world can do,
Or the weapons or faces of men;

As I walk alone with God's Son,
We seek our Father's Face;

We'll win this race, we must run,
Through God's Truth and Grace;

Ecclesiastes 12:7

For then the dust will return to the earth, and the spirit will return to God who gave it.

"At Our Master's Feet"

Convicted to a life in prison,
We seek to be paroled;

The prison is our body,
The prisoner is our soul;

We long to hear our pardon,
As The Spirit sets us Free;

So we may dwell with Jesus,
Who holds the only Key;

To be absent from our body,
So we may dwell with Him;

To stand before the Lamb of God,
Who broke our chains of sin;

We long to dwell in Paradise,
Where peace and love do reign;

To worship at our Master's Feet,
Singing praises to His Name;

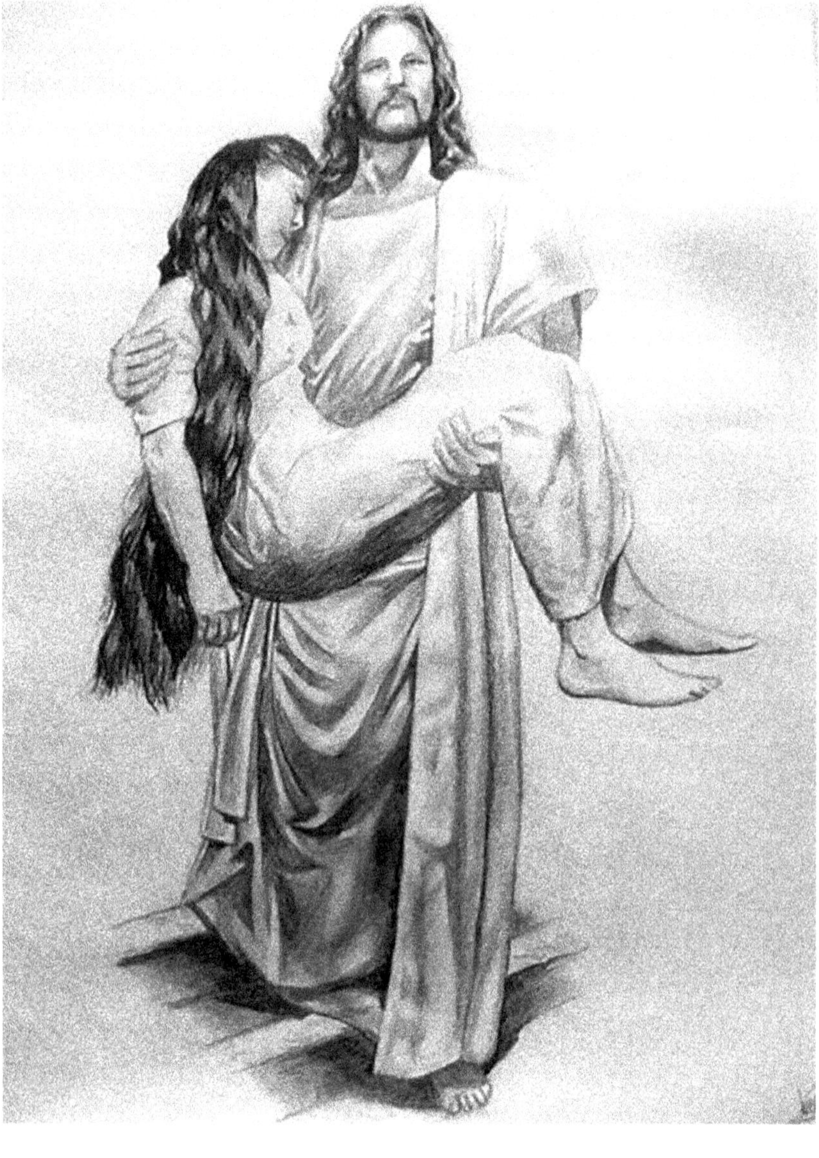

"In The Master's Hand"

Yes we stand, upon God's Word,
Without ceasing, Both day and night;

When the battle of life is over,
We'll know we fought a good fight;

We'll keep our eyes, upon the Lord,
Nothing will keep or hold us down;

For we who endures unto the end,
From God, will receive our crown;

We love to share God's Perfect Plan,
How Jesus died, and rose on high;

Our Life is in the Master's hand,
Need we say more, Goodbye;

Jesus

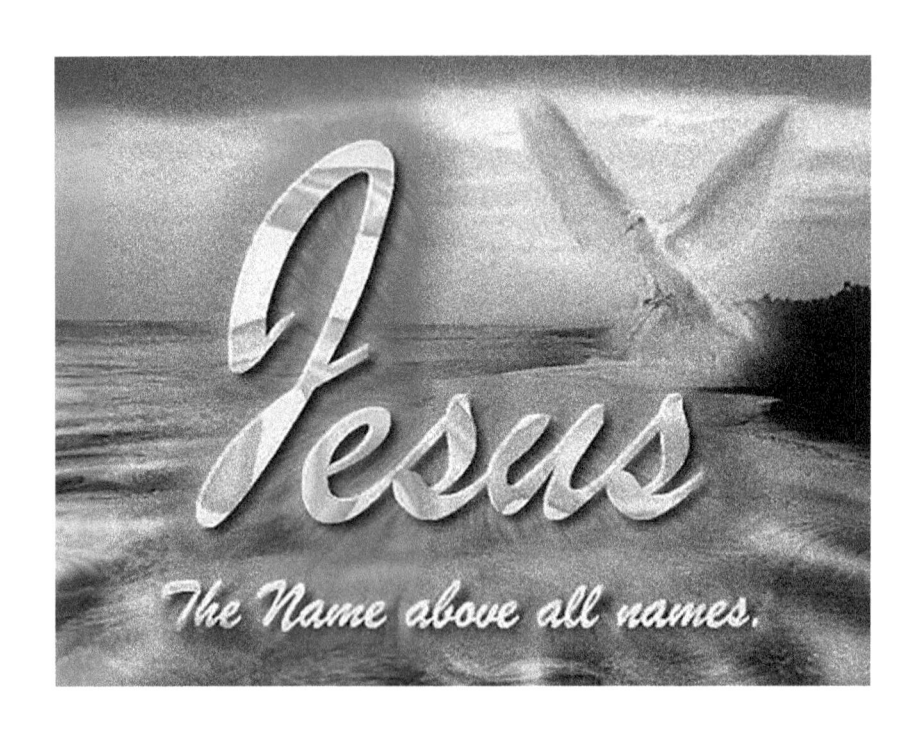

The Name above all names.

"To Jesus I Belong"

Greater is He Who is In me,
Then they who are in the world;

My heart and soul belongs to God,
By Whom the worlds unfurled;

I am a child of Almighty God,
To God alone do I belong;

When death comes to swallow me,
I will sing the Victory song;

"O grave where is your Victory",
"O death where is your sting";

For I will live beyond the grave,
To hear the angels sing;

Jesus, mold me into your likeness

"To Be Like He"

One prayer do I pray for,
One mission is my goal;

To find the lost in the sea of life,
A Fisherman, of all lost souls;

To be a Light, who shines in darkness,
His salt has not lost it's savor;

To taste and see His Word is good,
Ah such a sweet sweet flavor;

When I depart from this life here,
My desire shall forever be;

In me He'll find a perfect heart,
That I shall be like He;

* When we see him (our Creator, God the word John 1:1-3, Psalm 100:3), The Lord of lords and the King of kings (Rev 19:13, 16) The Lord of all (Acts 10:36, 37) As he is, and we will be like him, changed into his image and likeness, as God created and intended us to be (Gen 1:26, 27). In the image of likeness of the who bears record in heaven (1 John 5:7 KJV), As Christ like ones (Rom 8:28-30), The fullness of the God head bodily (Col 2:9) *

Well Done, Daughter!
Come...

"The Bride Groom's Wife"

If all my prayers, were answered,
If all my dreams, came true:

My mind within, would be transformed,
My heart within made new:

It's my desire, to be reborn,
By the spirit, sent form him:

To know and live, the will of God,
To break, these chains of sin:

To walk and be in perfect love,
To abundantly flow, with life:

To mortify, all lusts of flesh,
To be, the Bride Groom's wife:

* Christ, the word who is God (John 1:1), Who is the Lord of all (Acts 12:36, 37). He who bears record in heaven, is the second person with God the father and the holy spirit (1 John 5:7) is returning for his bride without spot or blemish (without sin 1 John 3:1-9). As we become as one with Him. Forsaking all for him faithful, obedient, and true to him, in sickness and health, for richer or poorer, for better or worse. *

POEMS ABOUT GOD'S KINGDOM AND HEAVEN

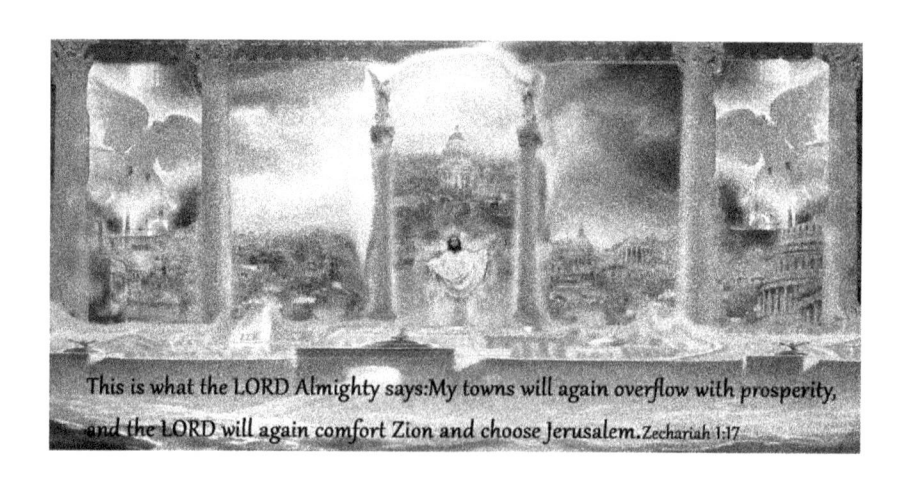

This is what the LORD Almighty says: My towns will again overflow with prosperity, and the LORD will again comfort Zion and choose Jerusalem. Zechariah 1:17

"The Kingdom Of God Within"

My Life and Faith abides in God,
For His Word, cannot fail:

He leads me by His staff and rod,
Through His Word, I will prevail;

He feeds me when I'm hungry,
With The Bread of Life His Word;

I need to search no longer,
For His Son I've seen and heard;

No longer do I search on earth,
For the pleasures or treasures of men;

For the Only Treasure of any worth,
Is the King and His Kingdom Within;

* A kingdom is the place, where a king dwells and reigns supreme. Reigning over all within His kingdom. The king of the kingdom of God is God. God is the word (John 1:1), Who is the king of kings (Rev 19:13, 16). The word who is God, is he who created the world and all things (John 1:1-3), Who is our breath of life (Acts 17:24, 25, 28), whom God breathes into one nostrils, into us, to cause us to become and be a living soul (Gen 2:7), God the word, the king of kings, the Christ in us (Gal 4:19, Col 1:27, 29, Eph 3:14-17), Who dwell in the kingdom of God that is within us (Luke 17:21) *

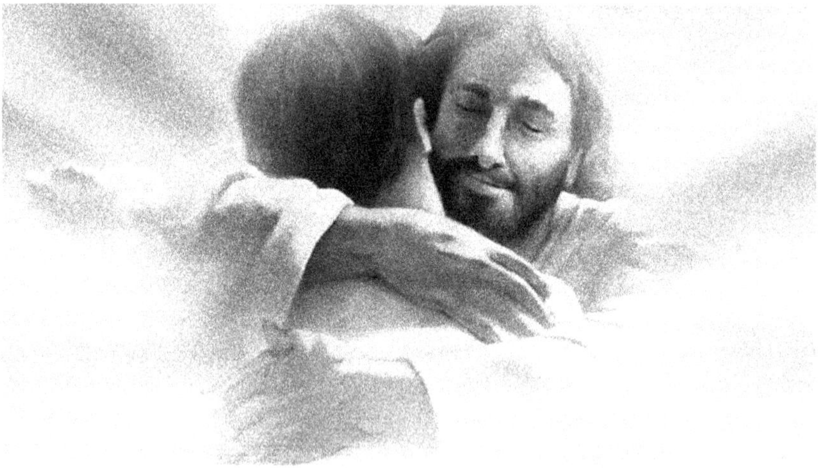

"A Place Prepared For Me"

When the angel of death comes calling,
When the earth reclaims my bones;

My soul will start rejoicing,
For the Only Home I've known;

This world is Not my home you see,
For I am merely a passerby;

My Lord has prepared a place for me,
A Glorious Mansion in the Sky;

Heaven's the Place, my heart adores,
The Only Home my soul does Love;

To heaven will my spirit soar,
Where my Father awaits Above;

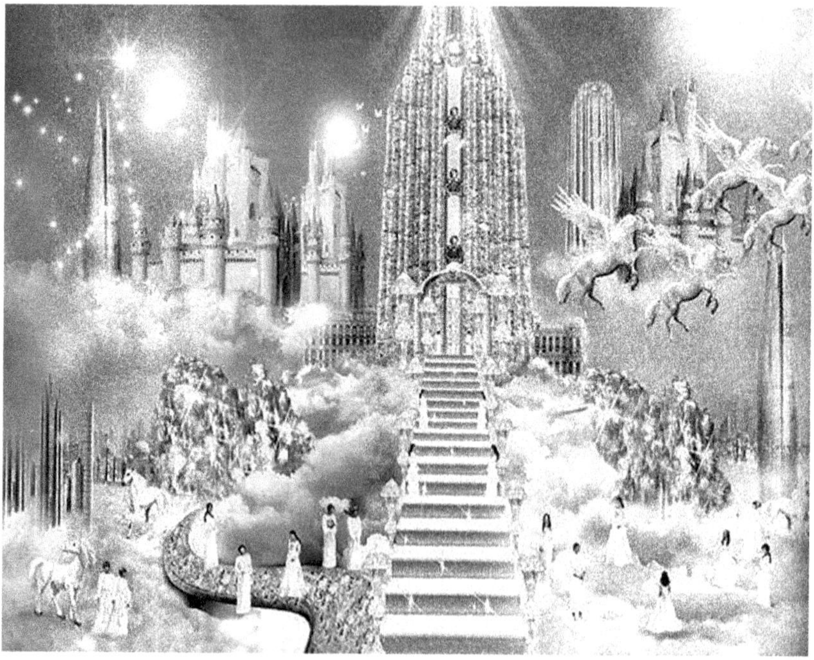

"God's Promised Land"

Unto The Lord we make joyful noise,
Unto The Lord we raise our voice;

Unto The Lord, we raise our hands,
Upon God's Truth we make our stand;

Let us be pleasing in God's sight,
As His peacemakers we fight God's fight;

Help us do what we know is right,
Guide us Lord through Christ our Light;

Lead us Lord where we should go,
Your Perfect Will we seek to know;

Let us love others as You love us,
In You O Lord we place our trust;

Thank You Lord as our Best Friend,
For of Your Love there is no end;

Lead us home where we belong,
In Your strength make us strong;

We walk with God hand in hand,
He leads us to God's Promised Land;

Lead us home by Your side,
Return O Lord receive Your Bride;

Do not be a prisoner of your past. JESUS has already set you FREE!!!

"Let Freedom Ring"

Let Freedom ring, Let Freedom Ring,
Upon All seas and shores;

For we are saved, by Christ our King,
We are Free, Forever More;

Freedom from the grave that bound us,
Freedom from sin and death;

Free through Christ, Who saved us,
Who is our very Breath;

When our Life is spent and done,
Our soul it will prevail;

Through God's Son, we known we've won,
Who saves our soul from hell;.

In My Father's House

"Returning Home"

When the angel of death comes calling,
Our soul says, Finally, here am I;

Our soul begins it's journey,
To join our Lord on high;

This world is Not our home to be,
We are merely passing by;

as we walk into Eternity,
Where we will Never die;

Reunited with our Loved Ones,
Who have gone on before;

In the place of many mansions,
In the presence of our Lord;

A realm where joy is always full
A realm of perfect peace;

A river of overflowing Love,
Whose flow will never cease;

A realm where the angels sing,
A realm where saints rejoice;

Before the presence of our King,
We hear our Father's Voice;

JESUS : "Did I not tell you that if you believe, you will see THE GLORY OF GOD ?" John 11:40

"The Perfect Day"

Each day is a perfect paradise,
As we walk and talk with God;

ALL our blessings numbered twice,
God leads us by His staff and rod;

Soon O Lord will come our day,
Our Father has set aside;

For us to cast away our chains,
The Groom receives His Bride;

This Lord is our's to have and share,
Your Love we Must Proclaim;

You're the answer to our prayers,
We gather together in Your Name;

When again we meet O Lord,
On either side of Life's bay;

We enter in through Christ the Door,
To begin The Perfect Day;

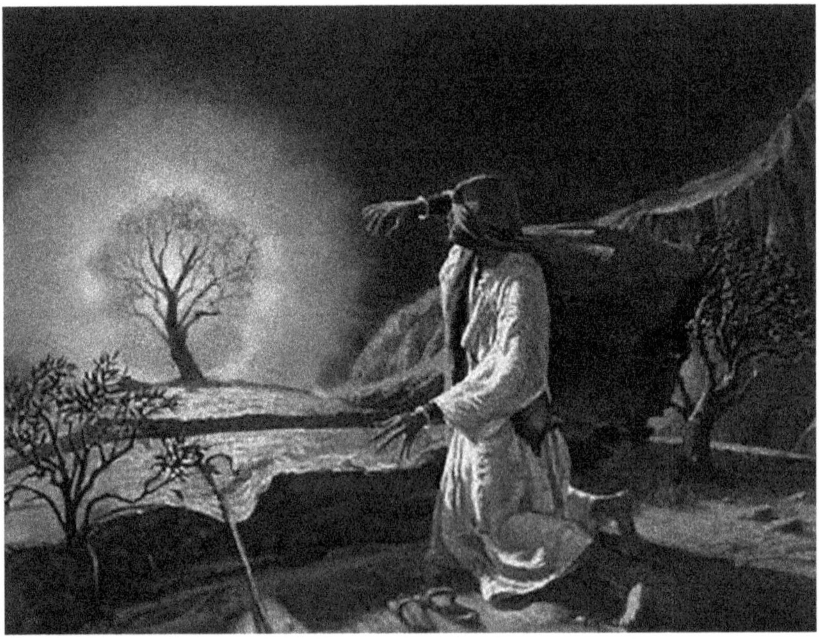

"The Tree Of Life Does Blossom"

Once we were deaf, but now we've heard,
Once blind but now we've seen;

The Voice and image of our Master,
Who is John One Fourteen;

We've seen the place of many mansions,
Where the river of life does run;

With pearly gates swung open wide,
By The Father and His Son;

The sea of glass, the street of gold,
The Tree of Life does Blossom;

Gold harps do play, the angels sing,
It's nothing short of Awesome;

NATURE POEMS

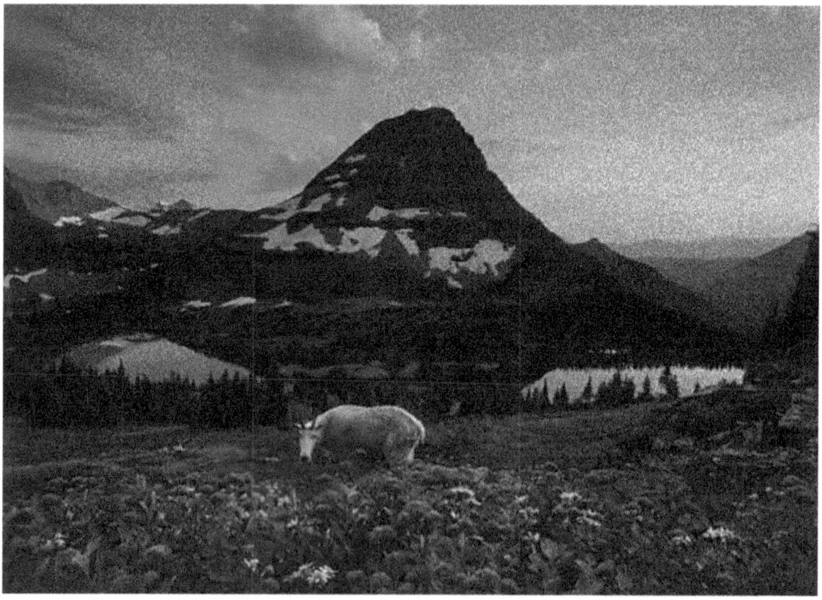

"The Handy Works Of Unseen Hands"

Ah the Majesty of God's mountains,
With their peaks so ever high;

With waterfalls like fountains,
Rushing down their sides;

That falls below to form a lake,
With towering trees around;

The soothing sounds the water makes,
Where God's perfect peace abounds;

The trees are swaying to and fro,
As to beckon and say hello;

All the splendor of God's Lands,
The Handy Works of Unseen Hands;

---

* The spoken Eternal word, the Eternal voice of God the father above, bears record in heaven with god the father in heaven above (1 John 5:7 KJV), is the word who was with God in the beginning as God (John 1:1, 2), The word whom we bear record of here on earth (1 John 1:1, 2), who is the lord of all (Acts 10:36, 37), who is the Lord of lords (Rev. 119:13, 16), whom God has magnified above all of God's own names (Psalm

138:2), who created mankind (Psalm 100:3), who created the world and all things (John 1:1-3), who was in the world (John 1:10, 11, Acts 17:23, 24), who is the brightness of the fathers glory (Heb 1:2, 3), to be revealed in us (Gal 4:19, Col 1:27, 29, Eph. 3:14-14, Gal 2:20) Our breath of life (Acts 17:24, 25, 28), God the word (John 1:1-3) in us (John 1:1, 4, 9). *

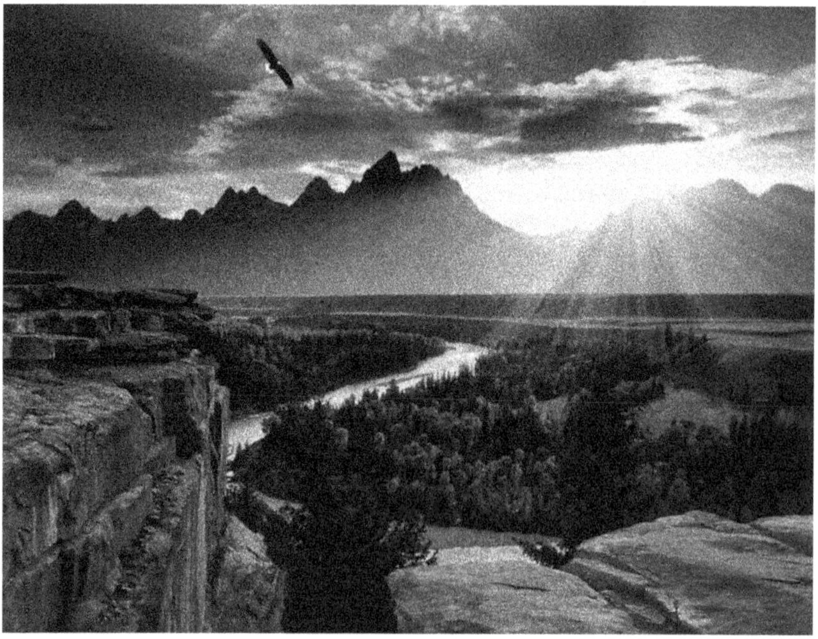

"The Tranquility Of Nature"

The sun is shining above mountain peaks,
   That forms a rainbow's arch;

All the peace, one's mind could seek,
   That stills the troubled heart;

High above an eagle soars,
   His mighty wings spread wide;

To gaze upon the mountain's floors,
   As he glides from side to side;

Yes it's such an awesome sight,
   It fills the soul with glee;

To behold, the moon at night,
   As it glimmers across the sea;

The joyous sounds of singing birds,
   The fluttering of butterfly wings;

A deeper silence never heard,
   As we ponder upon such things;

The hanging clouds like cotton balls,
   Float carefree through the sky;

I thank our Creator for this all,
   What a lucky soul am I;

We are God's workmanship,
created in Christ Jesus
to do good works.

Ephesians 2:10a

"God's Care Takers"

God He is The Only One,
Who creates His works of art;

Who gave to us His Only Son,
Who lives Within our heart;

Our Body, our soul, God's creation,
In Which God hopes to fill;

Through inspired revelations,
Upon God's Holy Perfect Will;

We're the Handy Works of Unseen Hands,
Created in God's image and likeness too;

We are the care takers, of God's Lands,
Which God made for me and you;

MISCELLANEOUS POEMS

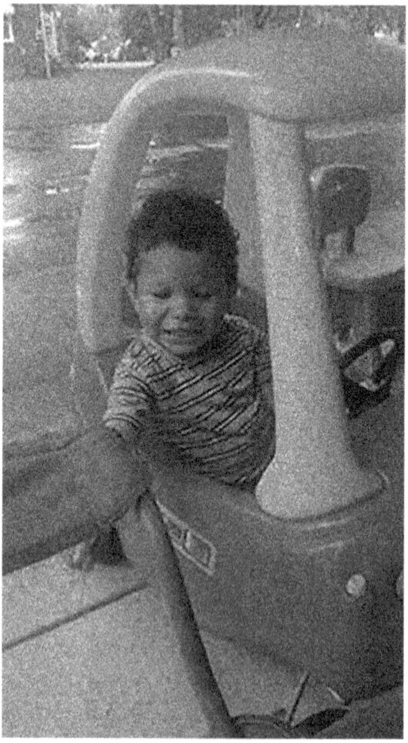

"The Simplicity Of Childhood"

(The Picture used for this poem is the Author's grandson Malachi Campbell)

When I was young and so naive,
Hours spent, playing make believe;

a walk in the woods, a stroll in the park,
Flashlight tag way after dark;

Rides down a slide, rides on my sled,
My loving parents, tucks me in bed;

A ready or not and here I come,
Hide and seek was so much fun;

"Now I lay me, down to sleep",
"I pray the Lord, my soul to keep";

Wish I could return to childhood days,
When all life required, was fun and play;

For there is born to you this day in the city of David a Savior, who is CHRIST THE LORD...
~ Luke 2:11

Merry Christmas

"What Christmas Is Not To Me"

(The picture used, is What Christmas Is to the
Author, Please STOP commercializing Christmas)

Shiny bulbs and twinkling lights,
Christmas carols, on winter nights;

Christmas trees, or a fire's glow,
Lots of presents, with pretty bows;

Santa Claus, or his little elves,
Christmas cards, displayed on shelves;

A mistletoe, or little red sleigh,
Lots of snow, on Christmas day;

It's Not about eggnog, or wrapping paper,
It's ALL about Jesus, Who is our Savior;

The Only reason, for Christmas fun,
God loved us so much, He sent His Son;

* Let every day, be Christmas Day in our heart *
* Christmas, a gathering together of Christ-like-ones, in the name of Christ, to praise, worship, honor, adorn Christ, seeking the fullness of Christ within us and through us. A mass of Christ-like-ones. The children born of God, gathering together to seek, find, know, understand, love, praise, and worship the only true begotten son of God, in the fullness of his presence. For in his presence, is the fullness of joy to the world, The lord has come. *

POEMS ABOUT SIN, HELL, REPENTANCE

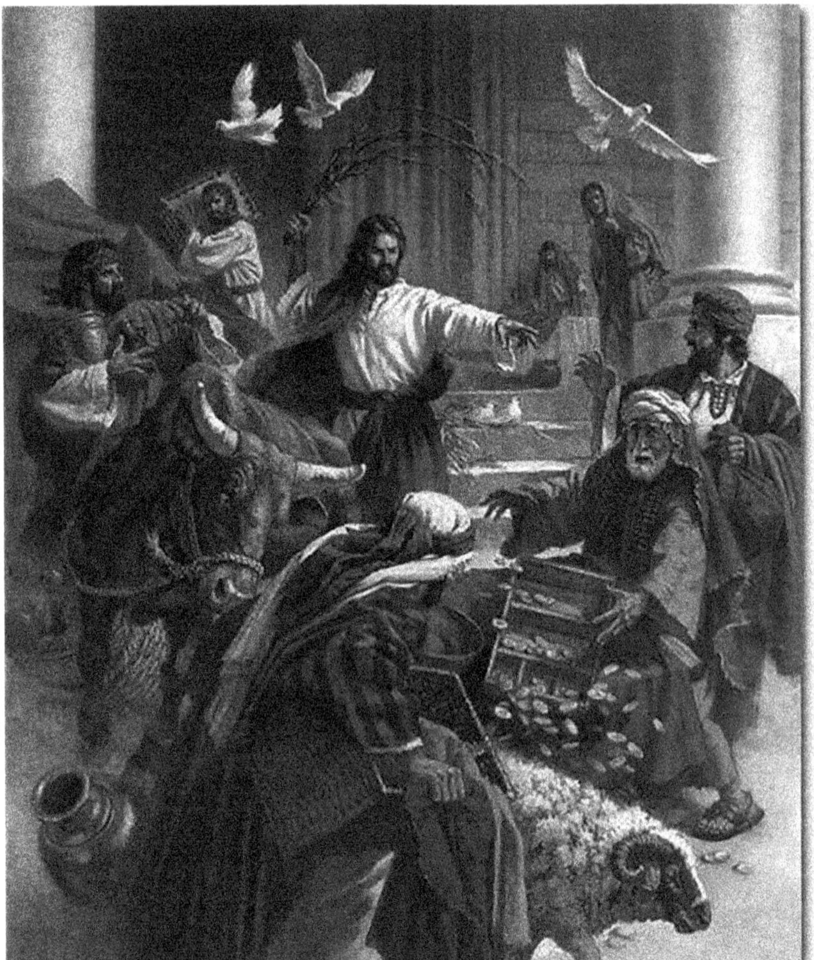

"For The Love Of Money"

(The Love of Money is, the Root, Seed
& Harvest, of ALL Evil)

God's command, to love God First,
To Love others, as ourselves;

In God's eyes, there's Nothing Worse,
Then Lovers of pleasure and wealth;

Those who use others, to become rich,
Judging others, by their bottom line;

These are they, who makes God sick,
Who sees others, as mere dollar signs;

For Money's sake, they lie and steal,
Some go so far, as to even kill;

How do you think, this makes God feel,
Do you think this is, God's Perfect Will;

*The love of money, riches, treasures and pleasures, more than love for God and our fellow mankind, is the root of all evil The root of the absence of God who alone is good. The absence of God is the absence of love, for God is love. The root of evil grows up and matures into a tree of evil, that produces the fruits of evil. These fruits of evil, is the forbidden fruit, we are not to partake of, that we are to seek not and love not (1 John 2:14-17, Col 3:2, Col 2:2, 3). *

FOR WE SHALL ALL STAND BEFORE
THE JUDGMENT SEAT OF CHRIST!

Least & great in the kingdom
of heaven ? (Matthew 5:19)

"The Secret Life You Lived"

(This Poem is about Hypocrits)

The Secret Life You Lived,
Not what you, pretend to be;

A totally different person,
When no one's watching thee;

God is He, Who knows you true,
He knows and sees all, from above;

He knows the things, you say and do,
It is God, Who judges us;

We will stand, before the Lord,
For Nothing will be hid;

As He reveals, before ALL the world,
The Secret Life You Lived;

* All that man thinks speaks, does and desires in the dark, in private, God will reveal and make known in the light, for all to see, hear, know and understand clearly. Even the very thoughts, intents, and desires in the heart and mind, of every living soul, will be revealed before all to all. Even every idle word that a person utters and speaks, that they will give an account of, on the day of judgment. *

Hebrews 3:13

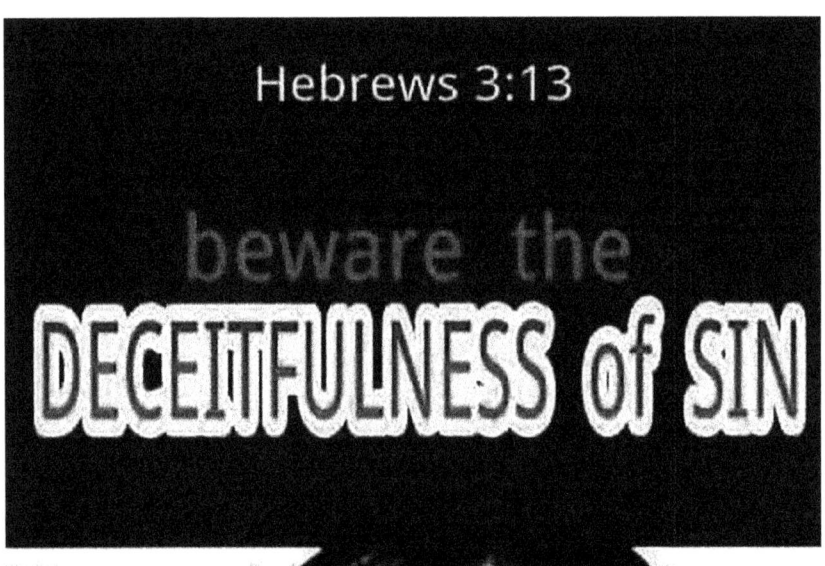

beware the DECEITFULNESS of SIN

Sin may give you what you want but you won't want what you get.

"So Silent Yet So Deadly"

(PLEASE NOTE; In this poem the Author refers to The Holy Spirit as a her. The Author knows FULL well that the Holy Spirit has No Gender, this is done only for the sake and purpose of Rhyme Only ! Just letting All the religious fanatics know, so they do Not freak out on the Author !)

So silent, yet so deadly,
Is this thing, which we call sin;

Temptations play their melodies,
Yet they thunder from within;

Sin it so lonely, yet so full,
Still it's evil heart does lume;

It's greatest desires, is to pull,
All sinners, to their doom;

Sing out my soul, your Lord does hear,
Unto the earth's four corners;

Cry out, for the Holy Spirit so dear,
And pray, that you may join Her;

Ah love the Lord, and love Him true,
With ALL your heart and mind;

Lest by chance, sin swallows you,
And a life in hell, you find;

People in Hell wish and beg for **SECOND CHANCES....** but its too late for them to repent

But **NOT YOU.**

"Heed A Sinner's Plea"

(This poem is about, a plea from a sinner in hell, to the living)

I had a dream, that I had died,
A nightmare, that I Lived;

For I awoke, my soul in hell,
For All the sins I did;

For I had lived, my life my way,
Without receiving, God's Only Son;

Now in hell, my soul must stay,
To serve the evil one;

Repent you now, All who remains,
And heed, this sinner's plea;

Pray to God, your heart be changed,
Lest you end up here, like me:

* Jesus said, I am the life (John 14:6), Christ who is the life came to give us life, more abundantly, and to set us free indeed of death. To set us free from death, which is the payment for, the wages of sin (Rom 6:23), to set us free indeed form sin (1 John 3:1-9). As we hide Christ who is the word, in our heart, that we might not sin against God (Ps 119:11). *

Today is the day of salvation

Everyone in hell would love to, hear an altar call, one more time. All hands would be raised. All would give their hearts and lives to Christ. For Real.

"Go And Sin No More"

I am because God is,
Because God is I am;

Without God, I am Nothing,
For my life, comes from Him;

Without God, I can do Nothing,
With God, I can do All things;

With God, my life has meaning,
For He is the song of joy I sing;

Let God be known, to all who breathes,
Upon the seas and shores;

For Christ has come to set us free,
Now go, and sin No more;

GIVE YOUR LIFE TO JESUS

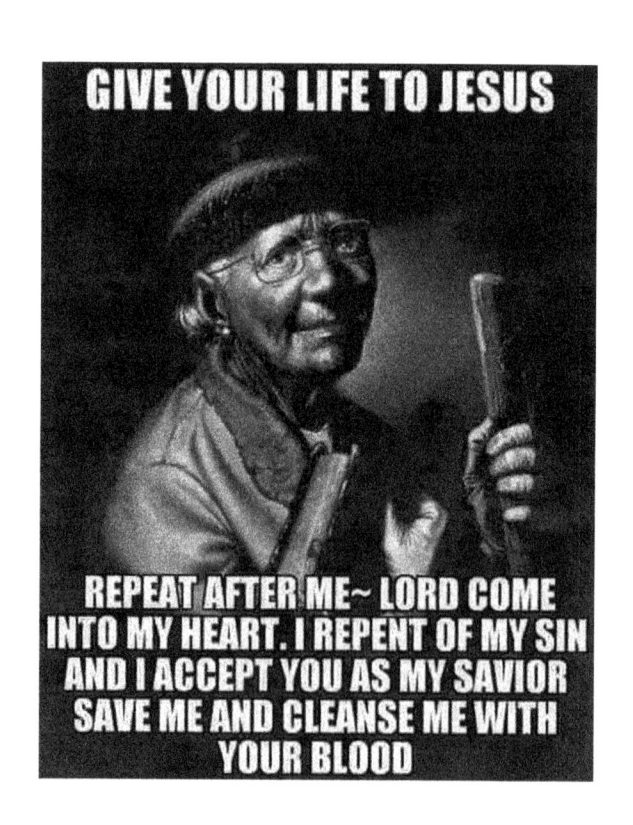

REPEAT AFTER ME~ LORD COME INTO MY HEART. I REPENT OF MY SIN AND I ACCEPT YOU AS MY SAVIOR SAVE ME AND CLEANSE ME WITH YOUR BLOOD

"Behold A Life Brand New"

I had my days of long long hair,
My days of drinks and drugs;

I had my days, when I did't care,
If I hurt the ones I loved;

I've had my days, of song and dance,
My days, of hot rod cars;

I had my days, of wild romance,
My fights in All night bars;

I had my days, of loneliness,
When no one was around;

It's then I sought God's Holiness,
For my world was crashing down;

God touched me, He changed my life;
Because I ask Him to;

Now ask the Lord, into your life,
Behold, A Life brand new;

(This was the Author's Personal Life, but Now is the Author's Personal Testimony ! What God did for the Author, who ONCE WAS a long haired, wild, ruthless fighting, heavy drinking, drug taking, marijuana smoking, womanizer, but Now is a Born Again, Bible Believing,

Holy Spirit filled, devil defeating, blood bought, faithful and True, child/poet/and teacher of God, God can do for YOU ! For God is No respecter of persons !)

The forgiveness which God gives
is full and complete.

"Forgiven And Loved"

O Lord I come,
Upon bended knee;

With heavy heart,
And single plea;

I ask Forgiveness,
For sins I've done;

I turned my back,
Unto Your Son;

Your prodigal child,
Returns back home;

I cannot make it,
On my own;

Forgiven and Loved,
Our Father proclaims;

Forgiveness and Love,
Are God's Names;

Return unto Jesus,
Escape All harms;

Father receives you,
With open arms;

Receive God's Son,
Sin No more;

For Christ Alone,
Is The Door;

Enter through Him,
To return home;

To know more joy,
Then ever known;

OH WHEN THE SAINTS
GO MARCHING IN
OH LORD
I WANT TO BE
IN THAT
NUMBER!

"Love Marches Forever On"

Love, the Completion of our dreams,
Love's Power, sets us free:

Love, Loves us, for who we are,
Not, as we ought to be;

Love, does Not think evil,
Love, only sees the good;

Love, sees past All our faults,
As only True Love could;

Love, can say, I'm sorry,
Admit, when we are wrong;

Love, says I forgive you,
Then marches forever on;

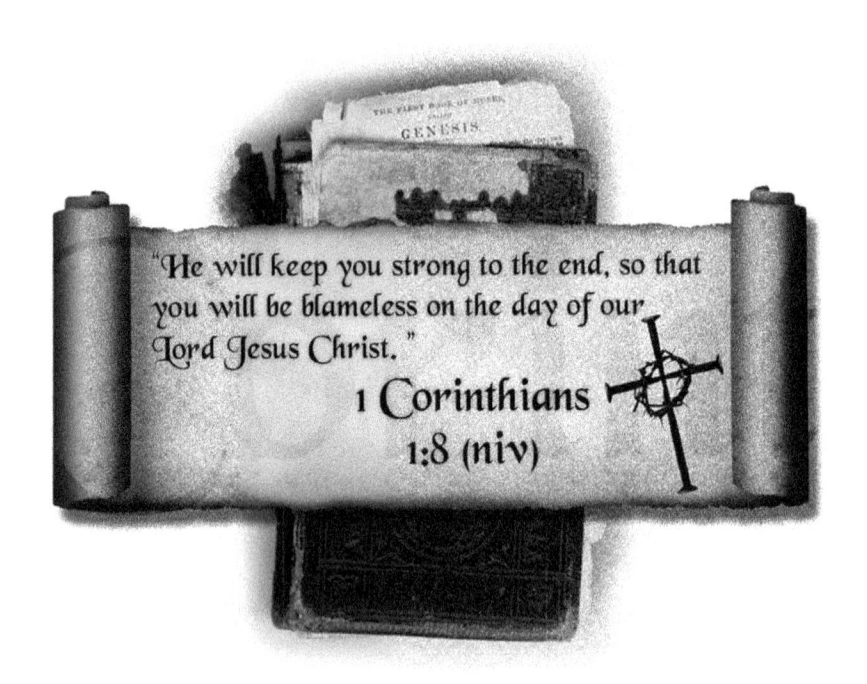

"He will keep you strong to the end, so that you will be blameless on the day of our Lord Jesus Christ."

1 Corinthians 1:8 (niv)

"Christian Soldiers"

Our Mighty General,
Is Almighty God;

He Leads His Army,
By Staff And Rod;

As Christian Soldiers,
We Never Back Down;

On Bended Knees,
We Stand Our Ground;

We Stand For Truth,
We Fight For Peace;

We March For Love,
That Will Not Cease;

We Have No Fear,
We Keep The Faith;

We Defeat ALL Evil,
Through God's Grace;

We Do Not Hesitate,
We Will Not Pause;

We March On Hell,
For Heaven's Cause;

We Shine God's Light,
In Each Dark Place;

To Save Lost Souls,
Of The Human Race;

Man's Salvation,
Is Not For Sale;

The Gates Of Hell,
Will Not Prevail'

We Will Not Hide,
We Will Not Run;

Through Our Lord,
The Battle's Won;

Greater Is Christ,
Who Lives Within;

Than Weapons Of War,
And Traditions Of Men;

No Weapon Can Prosper,
No Devil Can Win;

The Victory's Ours,
Over Death And Sin;

Thanks for being
my true friend!
It's a blessing
to have you
in my life!

"Let's Be Friends"

A Friend, is one you count on,
A Friend, is one you trust;

A Friend, is one you lean on,
When you feel like giving up;

A Friend, is Always there for you,
Through good times and the bad;

A Friend, is there to cheer you up,
When your heart is broke or sad;

A Friend, knows All your secrets,
But Who Never repeats a one;

A Friend, will Never judge you,
For Any wrongs you've done;

A Friend, knows your Every fear,
Who calms your troubled soul;

A Friend, knows your Every dream,
Who makes your life feel whole;

Not a mistake
Not a problem
Not a burden
Not an inconvenience
Not a nuisance
Not an accident
Not a punishment
A MIRACLE

"Protect The Unborn"

All Life Begins,
In God's Heart:

Before The Womb,
All Life Starts:

Before The Womb,
God Knew Us:

Within The Womb,
God Formed Us:

ALL The Unborn,
God Truly Loves:

Our Precious Gifts,
From God Above;

Do NOT Destroy,
Life God Makes;

Girls And Boys,
Whom God Creates:

Stop Senseless Killings,
Of Innocent Babes:

They Are Our Future,
Conceived Today:

Let Them Be Born,
As We Have Been:

Protect God's Gifts,
Received From Him:

For God Is He,
Who Gives Them Breath,
'
So Who Are We,
To Cause Their Death:

You Shall NOT Kill,
Our Lord Commands:

Stop The Abortions,
That Plagues Our Lands;

We Will Stand,
Before God Our Judge;

For Saving Or Killing,
The Unborn God Loves;

The Slain Unborn,
They Still Remain;

Who Waits For Us,
In God's Domain:

They Are There,
On The Other Side;

To Ask Of Us,
Why They Died;

How Shall We Answer,
What Will We Say;

Before Their Presence,
On Judgement Day:

Keep the Unity of the Spirit

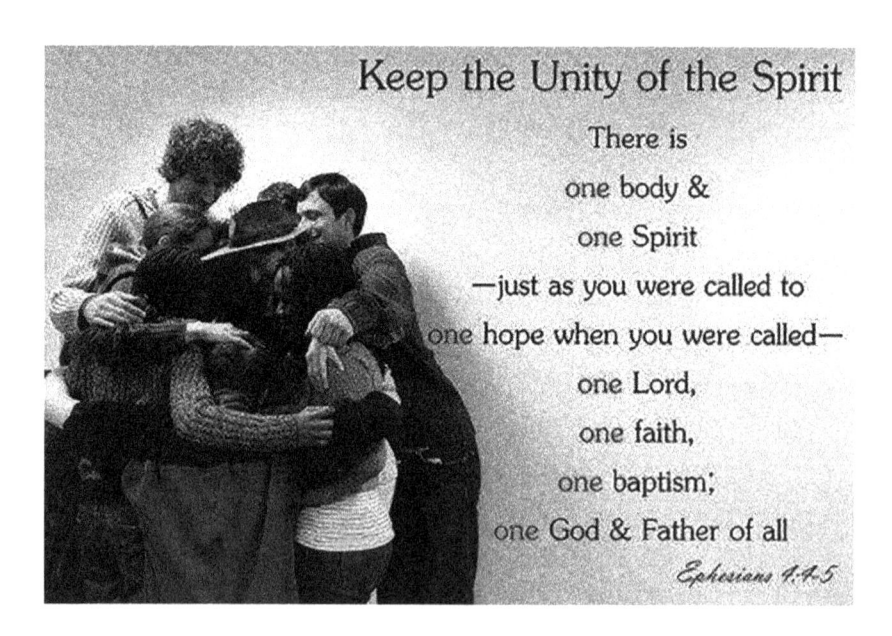

There is
one body &
one Spirit
—just as you were called to
one hope when you were called—
one Lord,
one faith,
one baptism;
one God & Father of all

Ephesians 4:4-5

"We Are One"

Let Us Set,
Our Color Aside;

Let Us See,
The One Inside;

Let Us Walk,
Hand In Hand;

Let Us Love,
Our Fellow Man:

Let Us Live,
Heart To Heart;

Let Us Strive,
To Do Our Part;

Let Us Work,
To Live In Peace;

Let Us Pray,
Divisions Cease;

Let Us Persist,
Until We've Won;

Let Us Remember,
We Are One;

"I Know that one day the breeze of love will come this way"

"Come here, I will show you The Bride, THE LAMB'S Wife." Revelation 21:9

"Homeward Bound"

Seeking, For God's Kingdom,
To Drink, From Holy Grail;.

A Journey To, Eternal Shore,
For Which, We Set Our Sail;

We Will Stay, Upon Our Course,
Our Faith, Will Never Waiver;

As We Seek, The Face Of God,
Of Jesus, Who's Our Savior;

We Will Reach, God's Promised Land,
As Jesus, Leads The Way;

To Stand Before, Our Father's Throne,
To Begin, The Perfect Day;

There We'll Dwell, Forever More,
Basking In God's Light;

Wrapped Within, Our Father's Love,
No More To Say, Goodnight;

About the Author

Author, Samuel Campian Jackson, preferred name Brother Boe, was born August 26, 1961, in Honolulu, Hawaii. He now lives at 23111 State Route 30 Minerva, OH 44657. Phone number 234-300-1243.

Brother Boe was born again, October 1982 in Minerva Ohio. After having the exact same experience of Saul, on the road to Damascus, seeing the same light of the world, hearing the same voice who created the world.

Brother Boe was married to Karen Sue Baker on May 25th 1999. A wonderful woman after God's own heart, a blessing to everyone,

Brother Boe's mother is Larraine Deloris (Campian) Jackson, born January 8th 1942. Father Samuel Dean Jackson 1-26-1941 - 7-15-2015.

Brother Boe has three sons- Courtney David Ramsden, David Andrew Streets and Joshua Emmanuel Gould.

Brother Boe has two daughters- Danielle Davina Tomlyn, Sheree Dowdell and Brittany Marie Gould.

Brother Boe has six grandsons- Hayden Streets, Jacob Tibbets, Berman Gore IV, Conner Gore and Malachi Campbell, and one grandson Carter Hayes.

Brother Boe has six granddaughters- Annabelle Streets, Sophia Gore, Lyla Gore, Madison Dowdell, Avery Gould, and one granddaughter Devyla Gould.

Brother Boe has one sibling, Deborah (Debbie) Dove (Jackson) Clapsaddle. Born 12-7-1965.

Brother Boe has one stepdaughter, Lisa Ann Theaker.

Brother Boe's Mother-in-Law, Mildred Baker, born 9-23-1925, age 90. More lively than a 60-year old.

Brother Boe has been disabled since June of 2006 due to severe spinal difficulties.

Brother Boe is 5'9" tall, weighs 150 pounds down from 245 pounds. A reverse Mohawk and baby blue eyes, and full dentures. Lol

Brother Boe's interests and passions are: God, family, friends, love and kindness for children, the elderly, orphans, the poor and the homeless, the hungry and the naked, and strangers. Also Brother Boe loves cooking, cleaning camping, hiking, reading, writing, learning, singing, dancing gardening, interior decorating, drawing and you.

Brother Boe is an extreme people, animal and nature lover also.

Brother Boe is an extreme hopeless romantic. Loves candle-lit dinners with his wife, strolls barefoot on the beach, walks in the park, hikes in the tranquil forest and laying down to gaze at a starlit night.

Brother Boe's hope and prayer is, to go into the world, to share and spread selfless love, perfect peace, abundant joy and truth that sets the captives free indeed.

Brother Boe encourages, invites and welcomes everyone to call, write by, snail mail, or to drop by to visit in person anytime. In hopes to build a loving lifetime relationship between the author and the reader, to share dreams, aspirations and inspirations, to share prayer requests and praise reports. To share tribulations and triumphs. To bare and share souls together. To invite one another into each other's home and life as family. To be open, honest and transparent with one another without fear of judgment or condemnation.

Brother Boe's next book to be published is "God's Voice Speaks".

Brother Boe hopes and prays that "Love's Voice Speaks" will be accepted and successful enough. That he can give free of charge, "Love's Voice Speaks", to shut in inmates, nursing home residents, orphans, and hospital patients, all over the world, as God loves a cheerful giver.